MEDICAL MYSTERY

MEDICAL MYSTERY

Richard L. Mabry, MD

TABLE OF CONTENTS

AUTHOR'S NOTES

I had no idea when I started this book that it was going to be more than "a book about a nurse who was trying to write in her spare time and a doctor who found love after his first wife died." It turned out to be a lot more than that.

I thank my wife for believing that I have one more book in me. I hope my faithful readers will agree that it was worth the wait.

I am grateful for the work done by Dineen Miller in designing the cover, and for the editing done by Kay Mabry and by Barbara Scott. Publication was carried out under the supervision of Virginia Smith, with thanks to White Glove Publishing. Any errors are mine alone.

As always, of course, *Soli Deo Gloria*.

1

The knuckle of the trigger finger was white with tension. The pistol was rock-steady and aimed at her chest. The person behind the gun smiled slightly. "Any final words?"

There was no way out. She wondered if she'd hear the gunshot that ended it all.

The cell phone in her pocket began vibrating, effectively breaking her concentration. Diane Macklin tried to ignore it, but it didn't work. Nothing came.

She turned from the computer and pulled the instrument from her pocket. Maybe a way for her heroine to get out of the predicament would come to her while she talked.

There had been a call from her mother about twenty minutes ago, which Diane ignored. Maybe her mother was calling back now, and, like all her mother's calls, it was probably of no importance. Well, perhaps this time it would be different, although she wasn't confident that her mother would change.

When she looked at the caller ID, though, Diane was surprised that this call was from her older sister. Unlike her mother, Patricia rarely called, and when she did it was because she needed something. Diane wondered what it was this time.

She pushed the button and tried to put a smile in her voice. "Patricia, what's going on?"

"Mom has just been taken to the emergency room. You'd better hurry over to check on her."

"What ... Tell me ..." But her sister had already ended the call.

...

The emergency room was a frightening place to most people, but a few found it as familiar as home ... maybe more. Diane counted herself in the latter group. After all, she'd worked there as a nurse for several years. She knew that lives were lost here, but there were also many of them saved. To the patients and families, this was a matter of life and death. Usually, for the staff, it was business as usual. This time it was a bit different for her, though. This time, it was personal.

Her mind was occupied with thoughts of what might be going on with her mother, and as a result she almost bowled over Martin Perry.

"Sorry." She said it automatically, before she looked up and saw who it was. When she identified him, she wished she could take back the "sorry." Diane tried to hurry on to avoid a conversation, but Martin had other ideas.

"What's your hurry?" he asked. "Every time I come here, I look around, but I never see you."

That's because I don't want to see you, Martin. Not now. Not ever. It was a shame that he hadn't just left town after "the episode." Instead, he'd remained, not just as a citizen but as a member of the local police.

She'd considered leaving herself, but after some vacillation, she hadn't done so. Diane had stayed, mainly because someone had to take care of her mother. Since Patricia was much too busy with her own life, the task had fallen to the other daughter, Diane. And when she thought about it, since she essentially had no other life except her work, it made some degree of sense.

Now, how to handle Martin? Diane took a deep breath. Maybe she could keep this civil. "Martin, I don't mean to be rude, but my mother has been brought into the ER and—"

He backed up a step, holding up both hands with the palms outward. "Oh, I didn't mean to delay you." Martin stepped aside, unconsciously shifting his holster as he moved. "Be certain to let me know if there's anything I can do."

Diane was already moving, ready to seek out her mother. She was about to bypass the admitting desk when she saw a familiar face there, absorbed in the typing and filing that was part of the administrative aspect that kept the ER running.

She'd seen plenty of instances where folks would spend half an hour or more trying to find a loved one who was supposed to be somewhere within the hospital only to find they'd been moved elsewhere. Better find out her mother's whereabouts for sure before she went off on a wild-goose chase. Diane stopped and bent over the desk, causing the woman to pause with her fingers still on the keyboard. "Sherry, is my mother here?"

Sherry Conklin looked up from her computer and a smile creased her cocoa-colored face. "Hi, Diane. She's in back—room B, I think. Doctor Adams is with her." Obviously trying to ease her friend's mind, she added, "Don't worry. Whatever's wrong with her, she's in the best possible hands."

After expressing her thanks to Sherry, Diane went through the double doors and headed for treatment room B. The "rooms" were simply areas set off by curtains, and at area B, the curtains were fully closed on three sides. However, there was a partial opening on the side facing the emergency room, and through this Diane could see her mother, lying on a gurney.

Ina Macklin was breathing oxygen through a mask, a pulse oximeter on her finger and wires from a multi-lead EKG going from her chest to the monitor behind the stretcher. A blood pressure cuff, deflated now, hung on her right arm, while an IV ran into the left.

Diane, having worked as a nurse in the emergency room for almost a decade, had become familiar with the readouts displayed in green above her mother's head. The pulse was slower than normal but otherwise unremarkable. Her oxygen saturation was within normal limits. The dextrose in saline running slowly via the IV probably represented just a lifeline, and thus Diane inferred that her mother's blood pressure currently did not need to be supported.

She saw Dr. Joe Adams bending over her mother, speaking softly. She guessed that he'd been in the ER seeing another patient of his when Ina Macklin was brought in, so the emergency room physician asked if he'd like to have a look at her, since she was also one of his patients. And, of course, he'd said, "Sure." That was what he usually did.

Most people pictured a family doctor as an older man—or less often, a woman— perhaps a bit overweight, peering over their reading glasses, fairly exuding reassurance. Dr. Adams had a great bedside manner, but his appearance really didn't fit the physical picture of a kindly old family doctor. Rather than being elderly, he was close to Diane's age. He had played linebacker in college and looked to her like he could still suit up. His brown hair was receding slightly, but no glasses hid his clear blue eyes. No, Joe Adams didn't look like your typical family doctor. But Diane was glad to have him there.

He leaned over the stretcher. "Ina, the cardiogram shows no signs of a heart attack."

"Thank goodness. But the chest pain when this started—"

Adams looked up at the monitor again before turning back to the patient. He spoke slowly, but with authority. "Your cardiogram doesn't look totally typical, but I don't see any evidence of muscle damage in the heart. You could have had what we call angina pectoris—a transient pain because of blood not getting to the heart. Your pulse is a bit slower than we'd like, but we'll just keep an eye on it."

"So, I can go?" Ina said.

"Let's wait until all the lab work comes back. But if it's okay, we'll just follow you in the office. I'll give you some medicine in case you have more angina." He then spoke to Diane, who'd been standing quietly at the foot of the gurney. "I think she'll be fine at home. And I'll call you tomorrow to check up on her."

"At least it wasn't a problem with my heart," Ina said, as much to herself as to the doctor.

Diane nodded. *No, it's not a problem with your heart. But it may affect mine.*

2

Joe Adams sat in the ER, studying for the lab work that had just been reported on Ina Macklin. Her cardiac enzymes showed no evidence of heart muscle damage. The only thing that was abnormal was a potassium level that was slightly high. That could explain the slow pulse. He'd have to watch to make sure there was nothing happening to boost it—too high a potassium level could be fatal.

Should he arrange for another day of observation to pin down the slow pulse and perhaps look for the cause of the elevated potassium? No, whatever was going on wasn't that serious. He'd simply follow her in the office. One of the benefits of outpatient follow up would also be an excuse to speak with Diane regularly.

He heard a sound behind him and turned to see Dr. Bob Carpenter peering over his shoulder at Ina Macklin's lab work. "No heart attack?"

"No. Probably angina, which cleared by the time we got her here and started oxygen." Joe Adams pulled out a rhythm strip printed from the EKG. "There's occasional irregularity to the complexes, and the rate is slower than I'd expect, but nothing definitive. Don't think I've seen an EKG exactly like that before."

"I agree. Going to get a cardiac consultation?"

Adams shook his head. "No. I think it's safe to let her go, but I'll keep an eye on her."

Carpenter grinned. "And on that daughter of hers? Right?"

Adams started to respond to what was apparently just some good-natured kidding but stopped before he spoke. If he was honest, he had to admit that when he considered Diane, which he'd done quite a bit recently, she did indeed seem perfect for him. Same age, medical background, attended the same church, unattached (though rumors circulated that she'd been engaged once). He'd asked her out one time already and received a very nice "no" but said in such a way as to leave the door open for him to try again. Adams intended to ask her again just as soon as he could be certain her mother's condition was stable. Meanwhile, he had a good excuse for calling Diane or even running into her in the ER.

"Joe? Are you with us?" Carpenter said. "Did I say the wrong thing when I mentioned Diane?"

"No," Adams said. "Just thinking. I guess it's time for me to get back into the game. Gloria passed on over a year ago, and until recently I never thought of being anything but a widower."

"Carpenter started to leave, then stopped and turned just enough to say, "Do you need to head home? If that's the case, I've got it."

"Thanks, but there's nothing waiting for me there. My life has evolved into a routine: heat up a Lean Cuisine dinner for one, go to sleep in front of the TV, wake up and change into an old scrub suit I keep at home, crawl into bed, then start all over the next day."

Dr. Carpenter shook his head. "Joe, you've got to break that cycle ... and soon."

. . .

Since Ina's transportation to the emergency room had been in a mobile intensive care unit, or MICU in the shorthand used by the personnel in the hospital, Diane figured she would take her mother home in her little Prius. They had left the hospital and were about half-way to Ina's house when Diane noticed a police car do a U-turn and fall in behind her. She was still wondering about it when the blue lights atop it lit up. Oh, what now? Diane eased over to the shoulder and parked.

Her mother seemed mildly interested, but not upset, by the unscheduled stop. "Is something wrong?"

"I don't know."

The passenger door of the police car opened, and Martin Perry emerged. His uniform was pressed with pleats so sharp they seemed ready to cut butter. Externally, Martin seemed to be the very personification of a policeman, including the utility belt that carried handcuffs and a holstered Glock. But Diane had seen the man inside the uniform, knew him up close and personal, and rather than the confidence his outward appearance gave, she felt ill at ease at his approach.

He leaned into the driver's side window. "Is Ina having problems? Need an escort somewhere? I saw you coming our way and had my partner turn around and pull you over."

Diane took a deep breath, counted to ten silently, then answered. "No emergency. We just left the hospital, and I need to get Mother home."

"Mrs. Macklin, everything okay now?"

"I'm fine," Ina said.

Martin touched his cap in a half-salute. "Sorry to have stopped you, but I guess it's better to be safe than sorry."

After the police car behind them was gone, Diane started her Prius and pulled away as well.

"What a nice young man," Ina said. "It's too bad the two of you called off the wedding."

Diane continued to devote her attention to her driving, her eyes straight ahead, her lips grimly closed. Since she and Martin, mainly her, were going to pay for the wedding, she had felt it was sufficient to stick with the story of "that's our business," keeping the details to herself. Diane had resisted at the time the requests from her mother and older sister to share the reason why the wedding had been cancelled. And she didn't intend to change that stance now.

Twilight was falling when she pulled up outside Ina Macklin's home, and Diane was surprised to see lights on in the house. She had made two calls after Joe Adams had given her the news that her mother would be going home: one to Patricia, who did not answer her phone, forcing Diane to leave a message, and one to Wilma, her mother's best friend and neighbor, who extracted several assurances that Ina was doing all right. If Diane had to guess who was waiting, her money would be on Wilma.

Sure enough, the door was opened to reveal Wilma Fairbanks, with Bruce, the dachshund right behind her. The dog was doing his very best to get through Wilma's legs and greet his owner.

"Ina, I'm glad you're okay," Wilma said.

Ina accepted Wilma's welcome as well as her help, and soon she was installed in her favorite chair, a rocking recliner that faced the TV set. She sat there like a queen with the remote control as her scepter, a satisfied expression on her face.

"Mother, what can I get for you?" Diane asked.

"Nothing, dear. I'm glad to be home, and I appreciate your bringing me back here."

"What about something to eat?"

"No," her mother said. "You've done enough, being in the ER for me, then bringing me home. If I get hungry, Wilma can get me something."

"Why didn't you call me when you thought you were having a heart attack?" Diane asked.

"I tried, but I didn't get an answer when I called you, so I called your sister. She suggested I call for the ambulance."

Diane was about to defend herself against her mother's scolding tone, but before she could speak, Wilma stepped closer to Ina and said, "I'll make you some more of my special tea. That should help you recover from whatever ails you."

"If you have any questions ..." Diane said.

"No, we'll be fine," her mother said. "Wilma will take care of everything."

Finally, after imparting a few basic instructions, including stressing that her mother should feel free to call her with any questions and promising to phone her in the morning, Diane took her leave. By then, the twilight had turned to full darkness. She pulled into her attached one-car garage and climbed out of the car, hoping that her mother wouldn't need her.

Presuming she was home to stay for the evening, Diane exchanged her jeans, tee shirt, and loafers for her old robe and bunny slippers. Should she fix something to eat, or just relax? She was just trying to make that decision when her phone rang.

Was her mother calling her already? Or was it Joe Adams, having discovered something in her mother's lab work he needed to discuss? She felt a sense of relief when she saw that the call was from neither, but instead, from her friend, Julie Anderson.

Their acquaintance had begun when the two nurses started working in the ER about the same time. Other than their professions, the two didn't seem to share much else. Diane was a petite redhead whose pale skin was dotted with a smattering of freckles. Julie was larger, her complexion was café-au-lait, and she wore her black, curly hair very short. But despite their dissimilarities, the two had become good friends, the friendship deepening over time.

"Hello, Julie," Diane said, snuggling into her favorite chair.

"How are you doing, Hon? I heard about your mom."

Julie was from the deep south, and Diane had finally gotten used to being addressed as "Hon." She was also quite often the recipient of some of Julie's home cooking. Actually, when she thought about it, she was surprised there was no casserole waiting for her when she arrived home today. That seemed to be another southern tradition Julie followed. Sickness, death, whatever the occasion, a casserole would fix it.

"It's been a busy day," Diane said. "False alarm at the emergency room. Mother didn't have a heart attack. She's home, now."

"Well, if there's anything Mark or I can do, just let me know. I started to bring you over a casserole but decided maybe I should talk with you first."

Diane grinned silently at the mention of a casserole. "That's fine. And I'd rather talk with you than have something to eat."

"Well, I'll get some home cooking to you soon."

As the conversation continued, Diane made the decision to find out Julie's opinion on something she was sure was going to come up before too long.

"Julie, how well do you know Dr. Adams?"

"Well, I've worked with him some. And I've heard the usual gossip around the hospital—nice guy who seems to have kept pretty much to himself since his wife died more than a year ago," Julie said. "Why do you ask?"

"We saw each other in the ER today, and I get the impression he may ask me out as soon as he's satisfied that Mother is fine."

"If he does, say yes, Hon. You're perfect for each other."

Diane nodded silently. "I've thought about it once or twice, but I'll be honest with you. My bad experience is stopping me from getting involved again. However, if I ever decide to try it again, it would be with him."

"I know about your experience, or at least how it affected you, and I don't blame you for not wanting to repeat it. But not all men are pigs, and if you need someone to change your mind about them, Joe Adams is the person to do it."

...

It had been a little more than a week since Ina came home from the hospital, and she had displayed no evidence that her heart's behavior was anything but normal. Diane had gone by daily after work, checked her mother's blood pressure and pulse, asked about symptoms. No problems. Other than the professional component of the visits, Diane had been hard-pressed to keep up her end of the conversation. Mostly, she just listened—which was the way her phone calls went with her mother, as well.

Now it was time to see what Dr. Adams thought about how she was doing. Diane had managed to trade shifts with another nurse, so she'd be free today for the follow-up visit. She hoped the doctor would say that her mother was as good as new. Of course, then she'd have to decide whether to proceed with her own life. But one step at a time.

She dialed Ina's number. "Are you ready to go?" she said, when her mother answered.

"Oh, you won't have to go with me."

Diane didn't want to argue with her mother, but it looked as though that was what it was going to take. "I want to. I'll need to hear for myself what Dr. Adams has to say."

"I appreciate all you've done up until now, but you have your own life to lead. I know you're busy, so I think I'll go with Wilma."

Diane didn't know what was going on, but it appeared that Wilma was the only one her mother would trust now. Or perhaps there was something between the two women that her mother preferred to keep from her daughter.

The conversation that followed was relatively short, and it appeared that her mother's mind was made up. Afterward, Diane sat with her cell phone still in her hand and wondered about the significance of what she had learned. On reflection she wasn't totally surprised that her neighbor offered to take Ina. The two women sometimes traded off on errands and rode together to appointments, and Diane was certain that she'd hear the gist of the visit eventually—if not from Ina, then perhaps from Dr. Adams. But why had her mother seemed so adamant that Wilma should take her?

Of course, there had been no mention of Patricia taking her. Usually, things like this—doctor's appointments, pharmacy trips, a follow-up to see if some minor ache or pain was significant—were left to Diane. Patricia's social schedule was always full, while her sister was an unmarried single woman who had nothing else to do, so why not ask her to do it?

Diane started to lift the phone she still held to put in a call to her sister. But before she could dial the number, she realized this wasn't the time or place to say what was on her mind. *Hey, Patricia? Why didn't you offer to take Mom to her appointment?* No, that wasn't the way to put it.

. . .

Diane didn't hear from either her mother or Wilma by the time she had to leave for the shift she'd traded to work in the ER. That evening she was helping Dr. Carpenter when Joe Adams came into the emergency room to see a patient. Afterward, when they both were free, he said to her, "When you have a moment, maybe when you're taking a break, I'll let you know how your mother is doing."

When she was free, she found him waiting in the break room. "Her check-up today was fine, and—as-you know—she's remained symptom free. Ina's potassium was a bit high when I saw her in the ER, but a repeat in my office today was in the normal range. All the rest of her chemistries and enzymes were fine."

"Restrictions?"

"None. Obviously, if she develops symptoms, we'll re-evaluate. Otherwise, see me for a routine recheck. I think your mother has the exact date of the appointment." Adams opened his mouth again, but after a second or two closed it without saying anything further.

Diane sat there as he walked away. *I wonder how soon before he'll feel good asking me out. And when he does—if he does—I wonder what I'll say.*

As she left the break room, she saw that Dr. Carpenter was, for the moment, unoccupied. "Dr. Carpenter, just between us, what is your opinion of Dr. Adams?"

"As a physician? Good man."

"What about as a person?"

He looked around to see that there were no eyes and ears nearby. "Social media has given us lots of acronyms. You'll hear people talk about 'wizzywig' sometimes. Well, that's Joe Adams."

"Wizzywig?"

"WYSIWYG. Wizzywig. What you see is what you get." He paused. "Although I don't know the details, I know you've been hurt in the past, and maybe it's turned you off from giving it another try. But, if you're thinking about dating someone, you couldn't do better than Joe Adams. With him, what you see is what you get."

. . .

Another week had passed since her mother's appointment with Dr. Adams, and she was still showing no signs of any heart problems. Diane was leaving work, looking forward to a quiet evening at home when she received the call from her mother.

"Mom, it's good to hear from you, but is anything wrong?" she asked. "I was just getting in my car to come home from the hospital. Do I need to swing by your place?"

"Well, yes—but not because I'm having a problem," said Ina. "Your sister and brother-in-law are here, and I thought it would be nice for the whole family to get together."

Diane thought quickly, and although she probably could get by with pleading fatigue, the call from her mother had an undercurrent of "you ought to be here." Her mother had no hesitancy in the past calling her at work for the most trivial things, but this call was different. Diane decided that something was up, and she wanted to know more.

"I'm leaving the hospital now and should be there in ten minutes or so."

It actually took her twelve minutes. When Diane opened her mother's front door, which as usual was unlocked, she called, "I'm here."

Ina's voice came through clearly from her the next room. "Come in, come in. We're in here."

Diane closed the front door behind her and went into the living room, the room they'd often referred to as "the room with the TV set." Ina was in her accustomed position, rocking gently in the recliner. The TV set was muted, apparently in deference to the presence of others, although her mother glanced at it periodically. Diane took a chair from the adjacent dining room and put it down across from the sofa where her sister and brother-in-law sat, and at right angles to her mother's chair. Patricia, and her husband, Herbert Norton, appeared ready to say something once Diane was there.

Herbert spoke first. "Diane, Patricia and I have given it some thought, and we believe that Ina should see the cardiologist that we recommend."

Diane opened her mouth to reply, but apparently Herbert wasn't through. "I'm sure Dr. Adams is good, and it's nice that he's found what he thinks caused her problems, but—"

She couldn't be silent one more second. "Wait a minute!" Diane leaned forward in her chair. "I saw that EKG in the ER. I talked with Dr. Adams at the time of mother's discharge from the emergency room. Her cardiogram was completely normal in less than 24 hours. She's had no problems since. Dr. Adams said she was fine—at least, that's what I'm told. Why should mother see someone else?" She was certain of the answer, but Diane would like Herbert or Patricia to go on record if they would.

Patricia sat silently, letting Herbert speak. "We simply thought that Ina should get the best care, and with my connections—"

"Your connections are mainly with title companies and the world of real estate, which is all you've dealt with since leaving law school," Diane said. "If you had concerns, why didn't you contact Dr. Adams, or me, or even Mother? Did you do any of those? I don't know why you and Patricia have suddenly taken it upon yourselves to look after Mother now."

"Wait a minute." Ina had been sitting calmly in her recliner, rocking, listening to the back-and-forth conversation like a spectator at a tennis match. Now she sat forward and spoke more forcefully than Diane had heard in several years. "I'm still capable of making my own decisions. I appreciate this sudden interest in my welfare. I think Dr. Adams is a fine doctor. He can call in a cardiologist when and if it's necessary, but I will make my own decisions."

"Well, mother—" Patricia started to say.

"Patricia, I appreciate the interest you and Herbert have shown in my well-being. I presume it will continue, and I thank you for your suggestions. But other than a possible increase in the frequency of your visits, I don't anticipate any change forthcoming." She leaned back in her recliner. "Now, why don't you girls brew some tea and serve it with those cookies the neighbor brought me?"

...

As the days passed, Diane noticed that her sister and brother-in-law didn't show any inclination to increase the frequency of their communications with her, confining them as before to times when they needed her to do something. She was willing to bet that the same held for their relationship with Ina.

Diane was just settling in with the cold chicken she'd taken from the refrigerator, intending to make it her supper that evening, when her phone rang. She heaved a sigh, but didn't even look at the caller ID. She figured it was probably her mother, calling to tell her something she'd forgotten during their last phone conversations (which had ended less than an hour ago). Trying to put a smile in her voice, she snatched up the phone and said, "Yes, mother."

"I hope you won't be disappointed, but this isn't your mother," came the voice of Joe Adams.

"Oh, I'm sorry. It's just ..."

"I realize you've been busy. But I thought things might have settled down enough for you to get out. You pick the night and the place."

There! He'd asked her. Now how would she handle it? What should she do?

She didn't realize she'd kept him holding for so long until his voice came over the line.

"I'm sensing some hesitancy on your part."

"I'm sorry. I was just thinking of some things." Like a diver poised on the high board, it was time to jump or back down. She took the leap. "That sounds great. How about starting with dinner? We'll see where the evening takes us from there."

"That's fine. Do you have any place in mind? And I guess we should pin down a night and time."

This was Thursday. She'd need time to decide what to wear. Maybe she'd do her hair. There were so many things, now that she'd started the process.

"Is it this difficult to pick a time?"

She had kept him waiting long enough. "Sorry. How about 7:00 on Saturday? You pick the place."

"Fine. I'll pick you up about 6:45." He was silent for a beat. "I guess your mother is doing okay. At least, I haven't heard otherwise."

"No," Diane said. "She's doing pretty much whatever she wants now." *And, since I don't have to spend all my free time running errands for her—so am I. I guess this is the first step in reclaiming my life..*

3

Diane slept through the alarm the next morning, the first time she'd done that since college. As a result, her phone call to her mother was quite short. Because she was in a hurry, she decided not to get into her date with Joe. Her mother would undoubtedly have questions, as well as comments, and she wasn't prepared for them. "Mom, I have to get going or I'll be late to work. I'll try to call again, or even come by to see you, after my shift is over."

Once she was underway to the hospital, Diane glanced down to check her speed and noticed that the "fuel" light on her dash was flickering. She'd gotten so used to not getting gasoline for her hybrid Prius that the need had sneaked up on her. With a glance at the car's clock, she decided that she really didn't have time to stop at the service station and fill up—she'd just have to hope the battery power would carry the car without the need for the gasoline engine.

Diane let out a breath she didn't know she was holding when she maneuvered her car into a space in the employee's lot. She snatched up her purse and headed at a rapid clip for the double doors that led into the emergency room waiting area. Diane strode quickly through the waiting area, hardly noticing the people there. She walked into the ER, stowed her purse and cell phone in her locker, and said to Julie Anderson, the nurse she was relieving, "I'm here."

"Catch your breath if you need to," Julie said. "It's nice and quiet." She followed Diane to the door to the break room, where the lockers were. "Things still okay with your mother?"

"Yes," Diane said. "So far, so good." She didn't tell her friend, Julie, that she was going on a date with Joe Adams. She wasn't really superstitious, but then again, would telling her friend jinx it? She'd tell Julie afterward, if things went well. And probably, even if they didn't. But for now, she'd keep the news to herself.

Soon Diane was immersed in the routine of the emergency room. She and Dr. Carpenter, who was on ER duty, worked together like a well-oiled machine. Diane occasionally thought that her machinery could stand a bit of lubrication, but by and large, she went about her business without a thought toward her other situations—her mother, her forthcoming date with Dr. Adams, and an occasional thought about her status with her ex-fiancé, Martin Perry.

The routine was broken when a police officer came into the ER, carrying a child in his arms. Diane and Dr. Carpenter reached him at the same time.

"Her mother waved me down," the officer said. "She said her little girl was having a seizure. The child was stuporous but was breathing okay. Since I was there, I put the mother and daughter in my patrol car and came right here."

Diane motioned to the empty gurney in treatment area A, and the policeman laid the child down. The child looked to be about 3 years of age. She was limp now, not convulsing at the moment. Diane thought the little girl seemed febrile to her touch. She placed the patient on her side to prevent aspiration, then put up the side rails on the gurney.

The mother came hurrying up as Dr. Carpenter started his examination. When Diane tried to send her to the admitting clerk, she said, "Please. Let me stay here."

Dr. Carpenter looked up at the nurse and gave the smallest of nods. "Diane, check her temp. She feels hot, and her eardrums are red and bulging. This is likely a febrile seizure."

The child was still out of it—probably post-ictal stupor—and it was easy enough for Diane to check the temperature. "39.4 degrees Celsius" she said as she withdrew the rectal probe.

"That's about a hundred and three Fahrenheit," Dr. Carpenter said, almost to himself. "Get an ice mattress and sponge her with alcohol mixed with water." To the mother, who still stood at the foot of the stretcher, he asked, "Do you have a pediatrician?"

"Yes. The doctor is on staff here, actually. Dr. Kerry."

"Call him," said Dr. Carpenter to Diane.

"Her," the mother said. "Dr. Kerry is a woman."

Diane called Dr. Kerry's office and, after being put once on hold, explained what was going on. The doctor issued some stat orders and said she'd be by to see the child in a couple of hours, but to call her earlier if needed.

After relaying all this to the appropriate people and getting the mother and the child situated, Diane peeked into the waiting area and saw the patrolman who'd brought the child in was still there.

"The little girl's going to be fine," Diane said to the policeman. "Ear infection causing a high fever, and probably a febrile convulsion. She's doing okay now. The pediatrician has been called. But thank you for getting her to the ER."

As the patrolman left, another policeman came in—Martin Perry. "I saw Patrolman Silver's car outside, and thought I'd check to see what was going on."

"We've got it well in hand," Diane said. She started to leave it at that, but when she saw that the waiting area was essentially empty, she decided that now was as good a time as any to have it out with Martin. She kept her voice down, but although the volume was low, she might as well have been shouting judging by the words she said. "I've tried to make it evident by my actions, but that isn't working. So here it is. I don't want to see you again—now or ever."

"Hey," Martin said. "We haven't really talked. Let me take you to dinner sometime soon. I need to tell you—"

"Have you talked with Carrie about this?" Diane asked, with an edge to her voice.

"That's one of the things I need to tell you. It never worked out for Carrie and me. I'm still unattached." He looked into her eyes. "So, how about dinner. Maybe tonight or tomorrow?"

"Whatever you have to say, I don't want to hear it." Diane turned around, walked away, and didn't look back.

. . .

Joe Adams was as nervous as a teen-ager before his first date. He'd changed clothes once, checked himself in the mirror at least three times, and kept looking nervously at the clock.

He gave a start when his phone rang. The caller ID showed it was from Dr. Carpenter, one of his friends who worked in the ER. He was all set to say he wasn't on call, but it wasn't necessary for him to use that excuse.

"Well, ready for your big date?" Bob Carpenter said. He'd told Bob about asking Diane out, but not much more. And he was sort of sorry that he'd even told him.

"I'm ready. And glad you're not calling me with a story about some patient of mine who showed up in the ER."

"No, we've got it covered. Don't sweat it. But it's just a date. You've been on them before. Why are you so worried about this one?"

He knew why, of course. His wife, Gloria, had passed away over a year ago. He'd resigned himself to being alone ever since her death, but Diane just seemed so much like the perfect mate that he was beginning to wonder what he'd do if she turned out not to be the one.

"I guess I've forgotten all I knew about dating," he said. "But Diane seems perfect ... just like God sent me a FedEx. I hope she got the same message."

"I agree with you that Diane seems perfect for you, but you need to relax. God has a way of making things turn out right if we just let Him."

He ended the call and looked at his watch. Time to leave. Adams had looked up Diane's address and was surprised that it was a house, not an apartment. Then again, some people lived in a house. He had, until Gloria's death. Now the way he was living, even his arrangements, seemed normal to him, and everything else was strange. *I guess it really is time for me to adjust some things.*

Diane met him at the door of her home.

"I have dinner reservations for us," and he named one of the nicest restaurants in town. "I hope that's okay."

"I'd be happy with a burger and malt somewhere," Diane said.

"You're much too pretty for just that," he said, then immediately wondered if he was coming on too strong. He really wasn't into this dating thing. Maybe he'd get better. He hoped so.

"Dr. Adams, I—"

"No, that's not my name. Not tonight. When we're in a social situation like this, it's Joe and Diane. Okay?"

"Sure. I'll try to remember."

"You'll try to remember, Joe."

Diane smiled. "I'll try to remember, Joe."

He wondered what other shoals and shallows he'd need to navigate tonight. There was a lot to this dating, a lot he'd forgotten. But he figured it was worth it if Diane agreed to see him again. And after that ... Who knows?

...

Diane sipped from her glass of iced tea and wished for just a second that she was drinking something stronger. She felt that, if any situation called for a stiff belt, this one did. She fidgeted and straightened the already-straight silverware at her place. *For goodness' sake, girl, get it together. You're acting like a teen-ager on her first date.*

She wasn't so far wrong. Diane hadn't dated for years—not since she had first gone out with Martin. But Joe was nothing like

Martin … so far. But she was still getting to know him. She had much more to learn.

Conversation, once it got beyond the initial stage of uncertainty, flowed fairly easily. After a bit of coaxing, Joe had told her his history—how he'd met Gloria, their brief but happy marriage, their plans for the future.

"Then, the diagnosis of cancer changed all that," he said. "I couldn't believe what I was hearing. I was a doctor. My family was bullet-proof, the same as I was. We didn't get news like this. I sometimes had to deliver it, but getting it—well, that just didn't happen." But they had gotten it, although he had a hard time accepting it. He'd gotten second and third opinions from the best people in the field, spared no expense or effort on her behalf, but to no avail. She died.

Diane reached to cover his hand. "I'm so very sorry, Joe."

"I sold the house to get past all the memories it held. Now I live a bachelor existence in an apartment." He hesitated, and Diane could tell he was deciding whether to go further. "I haven't dated since then—didn't even think of it— until I met you. You seemed so perfect for me. It couldn't be so right. But so far, it is."

Diane looked up from her study of the white tablecloth. It was her turn. But before she could speak, the waiter reappeared and began to clear the dishes she and Joe had in front of them.

"Anything more?" he asked.

In answer to Joe's look, Diane shook her head. "Nothing more." He held up his plastic. "Here's my credit card—add 20% for yourself and leave us alone for the next 20 minutes or so. Okay?"

The waiter nodded. "Certainly, sir. And thank you."

Diane was still absorbed in the moment, deciding how much to tell Joe when he said, "Now, you were about to say …"

She hesitated. "I'll start several years ago. I'd been working in the ER for about a year when I met Martin Perry."

"The policeman," Joe said.

"Yes. He asked me out, but I didn't think it was fair to leave mother alone. Patricia had been married about a year before, and my father had just passed away, so I was the only one around for my mother to lean on. So, when he asked me out, I turned him down."

"I know the feeling," said Joe, under his breath.

"He kept asking me, and I guess that Martin finally wore me down. So, I finally relented. After that, I suppose you could say he swept me off my feet. It took about six months or so, but he finally proposed, and I accepted."

"And your mother liked him?"

"Mother liked Martin, and even after we called off the wedding, he seemed to get along with her. Oh, I suspect that, perhaps subconsciously, she hated to lose her unmarried younger daughter who was always available to run errands for her. On the other hand, I think she was also glad to get me started on the road to a family of my own."

"Okay. So far, so good."

Diane looked down at the white tablecloth. "Here's where it begins to go awry. I was living in an apartment, but about eight weeks before the wedding date Martin said he'd found a house that was just right for us. He couldn't get out of his lease early, but why didn't I take it and move in right then? He'd follow after we were married."

"Did Martin move in with you? Did he sleep there?"

She was silent for a moment before she replied in a quiet voice, "Yes"

"I'm not surprised. And I'm guessing that's not what got to you. At least, not all of it. Then what happened?"

Diane looked at the trim along the ceiling, avoiding Joe's gaze. "From the moment I moved into the house, I started receiving calls from an unknown number. When I answered, I got hang-ups. I thought about changing the number, but Martin said they'd stop. One time I hit *69 after the hang-up. A woman answered but broke the connection when I didn't say anything."

"And did the calls stop?"

She gave her head a small shake, "No, although they slowed down. I asked Martin about it again, trying not to nag, but being persistent. Finally, about two weeks before we were to be married, he admitted they were from his high school sweetheart. He'd given her that number She'd never given up on him, even after he started seeing me—even after she knew we were about to be married. And he apparently never gave up on her, either."

"So, he was seeing her regularly? Did that include ... certain privileges?"

Diane nodded.

Joe lifted his tea glass and found it empty. "It seems to me that he could have broken it off, told her not to call."

"That's what a normal person might do—just put an end to all contact. Martin's solution was a bit more inventive. He thought it would be nice to have another woman at his beck and call, even after we were married. Then he suggested that perhaps he could get the three of us together for ... I can't say it." Diane took a deep breath. "At that point, I called off the wedding."

"Didn't you see any other signs, either before or after that?"

"In retrospect, but I guess I was so in love that I ignored his working late, his getting calls at our house, the secretive ways he behaved sometime."

"But you finally got wise," he said.

Diane looked up, and there were tears in her eyes. "He didn't contact me for a while after I called off the wedding. My previous apartment had been rented, and I'd already moved into the house, so I decided to stay there. I changed the phone number and locks, of course, and I had no further problems with Carrie calling me."

"Was your name on the mortgage?"

"He didn't sign for anything. He said it was because he had bad credit, but that might just have been an excuse." She drained the last iced tea from her glass. "I don't know what his plans were, but whatever they were, I didn't want to be a part of them."

"So that's why ..."

She took several deep breaths. "Yes. Now maybe you can see why I'm a little skittish about dating you ... or anyone. What's the saying? Once bitten, twice shy. Well, I was bitten once—badly."

"Just because you had a bad experience ..."

"I know," Diane said. "Everyone said you wouldn't hurt me. But he did, and I didn't want to go through it again, so I decided maybe I'd just stay single."

Joe looked up and saw the waiter approaching. "What did your mother say?"

"I didn't tell her all the details. I just said Martin and I weren't as compatible as I'd thought. Both Mom and my sister asked lots of questions, but I didn't tell them any of the details, and finally they stopped asking. I think my mother was disappointed because she kind of liked Martin."

Joe was about to say something, but the waiter interrupted with the credit card slip. He signed it and the waiter left.

"Are you sorry you asked?" Diane finally said. "Does this change your opinion of me?"

"Not really. It gives me a poor opinion of Martin, though."

"But not of me? Even just telling it makes me feel dirty. I don't know why I didn't see it earlier. I was so foolish. I shouldn't have let myself get in that situation."

"I believe any guilt you've felt is between you and God," he said. "And although I can't tell you how He'd react, there are all kinds of Scripture that tells us we can be forgiven if we truly want to put those things behind us."

"And this won't be a wedge between us?"

"I want to know everything there is to know about you, both good and bad. Nothing you've told me has turned me off. Of course, I can't learn it all on the first date."

She wasn't sure how to respond to that. "Are you saying ..."

"Will there be a second date? I guess that depends on you. I'm certainly willing."

. . .

The conversation on the way home was perhaps a bit more restrained than what they had engaged in earlier, and Joe wondered if he'd gone too far in asking Diane about her past. When they stood on her stoop, Joe looked her in the eye. "Diane, I'm glad you felt comfortable enough to share some of your background with me. And you didn't say anything that turned me off. Any feelings you've had about what Martin did had nothing to do with me. Get that straight in your head right now. At this point, I want to learn even more about you. How about it?"

It seemed that Diane waited for an hour before she answered, although it probably was only several seconds. "Yes, I'd like that. Why don't we set up our next date after you see what your week looks like?"

"Listen, I'm not on call next Friday night," Joe said. "Check your schedule, and we'll settle it tomorrow."

She looked right at him. "Are you going to be at church tomorrow?"

"Wouldn't miss it." *Not now, I wouldn't.*

Joe was trying to decide whether the evening should end with a handshake, a kiss, or something in between. Diane solved the problem for him when she reached up and gave him a peck on the cheek before turning away and disappearing through the front door.

He was half-way home when his cell phone rang. Could Diane be calling back to say more—or had she already decided to back out of their next date? Joe pulled to the curb and retrieved his cell phone from his pocket. The caller ID showed it was from the ER at the hospital.

"Dr. Adams."

"Joe, this is Bob Carpenter in the emergency room."

He was all ready to say something about his date when the voice continued. "I thought you'd want to know about this since she's your patient. The EMTs brought her in a few minutes ago. I think she's had a heart attack."

He was already taking a right to head for the hospital. "Let me head there. And who is the patient?"

"It's Ina Macklin."

. . .

Sleep eluded Diane—too much had happened for her to be sleepy. She lay in bed and thought about her date with Joe. He hadn't been turned off by what she'd done in the past—and, as she considered it, maybe he was right. Maybe she shouldn't be, either.

She finally got out of bed and made a cup of tea. It sat untouched before her on the kitchen table as she continued to think about tonight's date. When ending it, was a kiss on the cheek too much, or not enough? If he asked—and he essentially already had—was she ready to continue seeing him? What if the second date led to a third, a fourth, a fifth? Was she ready to move forward, wherever it took her? And, as always, the question arose of the effect on Ina of her no longer being available when she was needed.

Diane was looking at the kitchen curtains as though they were the Rosetta Stone for the questions that formed in her mind, when her cell phone sounded. The caller ID told her the call was from the emergency room of the hospital. A glance at the kitchen clock told her it was two o'clock in the morning.

Why were they calling so early? Had someone called in to say they wouldn't be able to make it to work this morning? Should she say 'yes,' even though she was supposed to be off? That would take her off the hook so far as giving Joe his answer at church this morning. On the other hand, was it just kicking the can further down the road?

Of course, maybe Joe had been involved in an accident on the way home. Or perhaps he'd been called to the ER for some emergency?

Diane wasn't finished writing scenarios in her head, but she needed to answer the call. "Diane Macklin."

"Diane, this is Joe. I'm sorry to call you in the middle of the night, but you and your sister need to know this."

Her mother. It had to be her mother. The thought caused an alarm bell to ring in her brain. "Joe, what's wrong?"

"Your mother was brought here by ambulance at about eleven o'clock tonight. Dr. Carpenter was working, and he let me know less than an hour after she arrived. Cutting to the chase, her EKG showed an early coronary infarction—that is, she was getting some heart damage. We did an angiogram and the cardiologist on call placed a couple of stents. She's stable now, and I think she's going to be okay."

Diane got up from the kitchen table and dumped her tea in the sink. "I'll be there as soon as I can."

Joe's voice was calming. "Don't have an accident getting here. She's in recovery now. Notify your sister, then come on. You can probably see your mother in a couple of hours."

Diane was about to hang up when she thought of one more question to ask. "Did Mother call the ambulance herself?"

"No," he said. "Wilma Fairbanks made the call. She rode with your mother in the ambulance."

As she dressed hurriedly, Diane's thoughts were mainly of self-blame. *I wonder why Wilma made the call. Why not call Patricia or me? Did Mother even try to call us?*

Diane drove through the darkened streets, her cell phone held closely to her ear, her eyes darting right and left as she tried to divide her attention between the phone call and driving. *Come on, Patricia. Answer the phone.* She had dialed her sister's number twice, hanging up each time after the allotted number of rings expired and voicemail kicked in. Diane hadn't left a message the first two times—that just seemed too impersonal—and it seemed that her call might go unanswered again. She counted the rings. Three. Four. Fi—

"Hello?"

Finally. Her sister sounded sleepy, which was understandable, she guessed, given the hour. "Patricia, this is Diane. Mother is at the hospital. She's had a coronary. Joe Adams saw her, and she's——"

"Whoa. Let me wake up so I can understand what you're talking about." There was the sound of the phone being put down on a hard surface—probably the table beside Patricia's bed. Diane continued to drive, silently fuming at her sister. Was the reason she hadn't answered the first two times been because she'd taken something for sleep—or been drinking?

"Okay. I'm back. Now what's this about Mom having a heart attack?"

Diane filled in her sister as her car neared the hospital. She considered parking in the staff lot, then decided she'd better put her car in the emergency room lot—she could move it later. "Are you coming to the hospital?"

"I'm ... I'm not sure. If you're with her ..."

"I'm in the parking lot right now, about to go inside. I'll either be in the recovery waiting room or with her in the ICU. It shouldn't be hard to find me."

"But she's okay for now?"

Diane breathed out through her nose, trying not to turn it into a snort. Typical Patricia—leave it up to her younger sister to do what's needed. "She's fine so far. If you don't come out now, I'll call you after I see her."

. . .

Joe Adams stood at Ina Macklin's bedside in the Recovery Room. She had come through the angiogram and stent insertion "without a blip," as the anesthesiologist put it. She was already starting to wake up, although she was not yet ready for transfer. Joe looked at the electronic display above her bed which showed the cardiogram along with other information. He was encouraged that the green lines of the tracing showed a normal rhythm to her heartbeat and normal complexes, with no evidence that indicated damage to the heart muscle. Now if there were no late complications. He said a silent prayer to that effect.

He sensed, more than saw, someone at his side. "Everything okay?" Diane asked.

Joe turned away from the patient, who was still groggy from the anesthesia. He held up both hands with crossed fingers. "So far. And in addition, I'm sending up prayers."

"Me, too," said Diane.

"Did you see Wilma Fairbanks? She rode in the ambulance with your mother."

"I came through the back way," Diane said. "Sort of bypassed the waiting room. I guess I'd better talk with her."

"I've seen her briefly, and told her Ina came through the procedure fine," Joe said. "But I'm sure she'd like to talk with you as well."

Diane nodded. "I'll go see her. And I probably should call Patricia, too, if she isn't here by now."

"The cardiologist and I anticipate keeping your mother in the ICU until we're satisfied that she's stable." He looked at his watch. "She'll have a follow-up cardiogram as well as some cardiac enzymes—" He consulted the clock on the wall. "We'll do those in a few hours. If she's doing well, she should be okay to go home soon."

"Did something . . . I mean, what do you think . . ."

"If you're wondering about something setting this off, she didn't give me any clues. I guess that's another reason for you to check with Wilma, now that things have settled down."

. . .

Diane found Wilma asleep in the corner of the waiting room, a magazine open in her lap. Before she woke the woman, she should try Patricia again. She moved to the farthest part of the room, which was otherwise empty, and made her call. Her watch indicated that more than an hour had passed since their last conversation. The call was answered on the third ring.

"Patricia. Mother's doing okay, and things are going well here at the hospital. Are you coming?"

"I was going to leave soon. But it sounds like I can take my time."

"Well, don't have an accident rushing here." She heard the sarcasm in her voice and hurried on. "We'll either be in the ICU or in a regular room—if she continues to do well, probably the latter. They can help you find it if you ask at the desk downstairs."

When she ended the call, she looked across the waiting room and saw that Wilma was now awake. She answered the unspoken question in the woman's eyes with, "She's doing fine." When Diane saw that Wilma wasn't going back so sleep, she said, "And how are you doing?"

Wilma had been holding it together fairly well, but the implied invitation to unburden herself broke through the dam and a flood of tears followed. Diane moved to her side. When the crying began to subside, she put her arm across Wilma's shoulder and murmured, "She's fine now. Did you ride in the ambulance with her?"

The crying had slowed to a manageable level. "Yes. And at the front desk, they asked me all sorts of questions that I couldn't answer, when all I wanted to do was follow the attendants into the emergency room and hold Ina's hand."

"I'll take care of those questions you didn't have the answer for," Diane said. "You did fine."

"Dr. Adams came out to tell me they were going to do some sort of heart X-ray, and maybe put in a strut or something. I didn't think I was the one to ask about giving permission, but he said that Ina had already signed to let them do it. Apparently, she made them hold off on giving her something for pain until she signed the permit." She used a sodden tissue to wipe her cheeks. "He told me later that she'd come through fine, but it would be an hour or two before I could see her So I've just been out here, hoping you or Patricia might come."

Diane wasn't certain how to ask this next question, but she felt that if she didn't do it, Joe certainly would, if he hadn't already. "You don't know what might have precipitated this, do you?"

Wilma replied in a voice that was so low Diane had to lean toward her to hear it. "No."

"You were with my mother last evening when she felt these pains coming on her. Why didn't you call Patricia or me? Why not notify the family?"

"Ina insisted we not bother anyone. I finally convinced her to try your sister, but Patricia must have been out. I wanted to call you, but she had heard rumors that you were on the first date you'd had in years and didn't want to bother you."

Diane started to argue, but decided that her problem was with her mother, not Wilma. She was spared further conversation along those lines when Patricia walked through the waiting room door, along with her husband, Herbert Norton.

Patricia wore a simple blouse and skirt that complemented the blue of her eyes. Herbert was ready for whatever lawyerly duties might come his way, in a suit of dark gray with a subtle pinstripe and a rep-striped tie.

The sisters embraced, Herbert gave Diane a peck on the cheek, and then both acknowledged Wilma, who stood a little way removed from the group during the greetings.

"Is Mother doing all right?" Patricia asked.

"When I left the recovery room, she was still waking up, but everything was going smoothly," Diane said.

Herbert was about to say something when the door to the recovery room opened, and Joe Adams appeared. "I see you're all here, so I can give you all the good news at the same time. She's doing well—well enough that we're going to send her to a regular room when she's out of recovery. In about another thirty minutes, she'll go to the second floor." He consulted a slip of paper. "Room 2300. The cafeteria's not open at this hour, but perhaps you can get some coffee from the machine in the waiting area on the second floor. The nurse will call you there."

As the group was preparing to leave, Joe motioned to Diane. "Could I have a moment with you ... alone?"

Joe flinched when Diane told him what Wilma had relayed ... about not involving her because she was on her first date in a long time. "How did she hear about our date?"

"That's not important now," Diane told him. "But for now, I'll need to be available for Mother on a regular basis." *Just like I've always been.*

...

Diane found the group in the otherwise-deserted second floor waiting room. Patricia and Herbert had Styrofoam cups of coffee from the vending machine in the corner and were huddled together conversing in low tones. Wilma sat several chairs over, her eyes closed. Diane approached her quietly, thinking that perhaps her mother's neighbor was sleeping.

Wilma opened her eyes and looked at Diane. "I was just praying for my friend. Do you really think she'll be okay?"

"Joe Adams thinks so, and that's what I'm going to hang my hat on," she said. "You know, I can take you home so you can try to get some sleep. I'll come by your house later and give you an update."

Wilma was shaking her head before Diane got the sentence fully out. "I couldn't sleep. Ina's my best friend—she's probably the closest thing to family I have. Other than her and Bruce, I don't have anyone."

Bruce? Then Diane remembered the dachshund that Ina had rescued from the pound. "Oh, yes. Bruce. Someone will have to care for him until Mom gets home."

"Oh, I'll do that. After all—"

Diane leaned forward, but before she could say anything, Martin Perry approached. Perry wore the nattily pressed uniform of a corporal in the local police department. He adjusted his weapon before leaning down to Diane. His voice was soft and gentle. "I was in the emergency room and heard about your mother. Is there anything I can do for you?" He almost whispered the next word, which he aimed specifically at Diane. "Anything?"

What Diane wanted from Martin was for him to leave her alone—now and forever. Maybe she needed to express that more forcefully, but not with her mother having undergone cardiac surgery. She didn't want to argue today. So, she just said, "Thanks for asking, but we're fine for now."

...

After Ina was moved to a regular room, Joe Adams stood aside and watched as the group fussed over his patient. Diane had been here the longest, but that didn't seem to matter. She was moved gently aside as Patricia and Herb established their position at the patient's bedside.

It was Patricia who, although the last to arrive, was the first to leave. "Mother, we're glad you've come out of this as well as you did. We're going to go so you can rest, though." And she shepherded Herbert out of the room and away.

Eventually, all the good wishes had been conveyed, all the questions answered, and Ina was left to recover in the care of the nursing staff and physicians. Finally, Wilma and Diane prepared to leave.

"I'll take care of everything at home," Wilma said. "And that includes Bruce. He's fine staying with me as long as necessary."

"If you'll wait a bit while I have some time with my mother, I'll take you home," Diane said to her.

"That's sweet of you," Wilma said. "I'll just make myself comfortable in the waiting room."

Joe started to leave as well, but a subtle gesture from Diane told him she wanted to talk with him.

"I'll keep Wilma company in the waiting room," he said. Ten minutes or so passed, time during which Wilma dropped off to sleep in the waiting room. Joe must have, as well, because the next thing he heard was Diane's voice, whispering in his ear. "Joe."

He awakened almost instantaneously. "Oh, sorry. I must have dropped off."

"You weren't sleeping very soundly," Diane said.

"It's a reflex, finely honed since my days in medical school. Sleep when you can but awaken ready for action."

Wilma continued sleeping through all this, and Diane beckoned Joe to move to the farthest corner of the otherwise-unoccupied waiting room so as not to awaken her. She reached out toward Joe but withdrew her hand before completing the gesture. "Now, how active can my mother be after she goes home? Do I need to take leave from work to be with her? Is she likely to have another heart attack if she lifts something heavy or exerts herself too much?"

"I figured since you're a nurse—"

"Remember, we're talking about my mother, not just some generic patient. So, I want specifics, just as though I'm not a medical professional."

Joe nodded. "Her narrowing of her coronaries was enough to give her . . . I guess you'd call it a 'mild' heart attack. I'd class it as just barely more than angina pectoris. I don't think there's much danger of her having a more serious one if she uses just a little common sense. And, no, I don't think anyone needs to stay with her."

Diane was quiet as she considered this. "I guess Wilma can check on her. Actually, she's probably going to be with Mother most of the time. And when I'm not at her house, I'm as near as the telephone."

Joe looked at his watch. "I think that I'll get a little more rest, instead of going to church this morning. But I'll be back after lunch to check on your mother."

"I guess I'll take Wilma home. Then, after some rest, I'll come back to check on mother, too."

Joe watched as Diane went over to where Wilma was sleeping and began gently waking her. He'd go home, but despite how tired he was, he didn't foresee much rest for himself.

4

After dropping Wilma off, Diane considered her options and decided that she wasn't going to rest at home, no matter how tired she was. So, she turned around and headed back to the hospital.

Her mother was now fully awake, and Diane's presence simply reinforced her feeling that, since her daughter was a nurse in that hospital, she should exert every effort to make her stay there more comfortable.

"I've tried to tell you, Mother, that there are rules and regulations, and I can't bend them any more than I have."

"But, for example, the TV set doesn't work like mine does. And it doesn't get my favorite programs."

When Joe Adams showed up, Diane tried not to sound like what she'd heard in the ER regularly—a person asking that the rules of the hospital be changed to suit them—but she told him, "She's not going to be satisfied until I take her home. And obviously, she's not going to act like someone who's just had cardiac surgery."

"No, and this is the best demonstration I can give you of her health. You don't have to baby her. She can do anything she feels like doing."

"So, when can she be discharged?" Diane asked.

"I'm going to have to keep her another ten or twelve hours, mainly to recheck her cardiogram and enzymes one more time. But if they're okay, she should be ready for discharge by late on Saturday evening."

By the time the final EKG and lab work were back Saturday night, though, Ina Macklin was snoring peacefully.

"She can go home," the head nurse on the cardiac ward told Diane, "But why don't we wait and let her sleep? Tomorrow will be soon enough."

Diane slept fitfully in the chair in her mother's room, and then the discharge didn't go as rapidly or smoothly as hoped for. Finally, around three on Sunday afternoon Ina was bundled into Diane's Prius for the ride home.

"I could have walked down to your car," she said. "No need to ride down in a wheelchair."

"That's the rule," Diane said as she helped her mother into the car. Was Ina going to complain about everything from here on out? Maybe she'd settle down once she was situated in familiar surroundings. Maybe.

In the process of getting Ina settled, Diane discovered a small white sack. Inside were two pill bottles. "What are these?"

"Some heart medicines that the specialist had them send home with me. I think the directions are on them."

One was nitroglycerine to use as needed for chest pain. The other was a beta-blocker. "I'll check with the cardiologist's office on Monday morning," Diane said.

Within minutes of getting Ina into her favorite rocker/recliner, Diane heard a knock at the door. *What now?* She answered and found Wilma standing on the front stoop. "I saw your car out front, so I took a chance that you might have brought Ina home."

Before Diane could say anything, Wilma brushed by her and went into the living room, where Ina was installed in her usual chair. She had the TV remote control, and was scrolling through the channels, apparently not liking anything she saw well enough to settle on it.

When she saw Wilma, Ina dropped the remote into her lap and gave her neighbor a hug. "Wilma, did you bring Bruce back?"

Diane, who'd followed Wilma into the living room, had almost forgotten about the dachshund who was Ina's companion.

"He's at my house. I wasn't sure you'd want him yet."

The conversation showed no signs of stopping, so eventually Diane interrupted long enough to ask if her mother wanted anything. Food, for instance.

Before Ina could say anything, Wilma said, "Don't worry about a thing. I know you must be worn out. I'll take care of Ina. I have some stew on the stove at my house, and I'll bring it over when I bring Bruce."

"Could you make me some of that special tea?" Ina asked.

"Of course."

Diane started to talk about how much Ina could do, but before she could get started, her mother said, "Anything that Dr. Adams told you about my care at home—what I should eat, or do, or anything—just tell Wilma. Or better yet, she can call you if she has questions. He told me I could do anything I wanted, and I want to just sit and watch TV."

As Diane got into her car, she gave one thought to whether she should really leave her mother. But Wilma seemed to have that well in hand—maybe too well. With a sigh, she started her car. The prospect of being at her own home was appealing more and more to her.

Before she pulled away, she realized that there was one more thing she had to do before she could let herself relax. She would need to call Patricia and let her know that Ina had been discharged.

As she buckled her seatbelt, she realized that, although her sister had shown up at the hospital right their mother's heart surgery, after that initial appearance Patricia and her husband hadn't been around. Could she have just made an appearance to solidify whatever hold she had on Ina's money? No, surely even Patricia couldn't be that cold. Or could she? And what about Herbert? Was he complicit with his wife in this?

Diane decided she might as well get it over. She used her cell phone to call her sister. As it rang, she wondered what she'd say. When the voice mail clicked on, Diane realized that she didn't have to deal with her sister right now. Instead, she left a message for her.

"Patricia, this is Diane. Mother's at home now. Give me a call when you can."

. . .

After Joe finished his TV dinner in front of the set that evening, he sat flipping through the channels, hardly seeing or paying attention to the programs available.

Finally, he snapped off the set and decided that maybe it was time to get out of the house. He'd check on Ina, see if she needed anything. Not really a "house call." Just looking in on her. Of course, if Diane was there, it would be another chance to see her. Although it was too soon to discuss their future dating, he found himself missing her when they were apart.

After slipping on his jacket and deciding that a tie was unnecessary for this visit, he climbed into his car and headed for Ina's home. He didn't normally take note of his patients' addresses, but he knew Ina's. Joe didn't want to think too much about why that was so—he just did. When he got to Ina's neighborhood, he first looked for the house number, and then for Diane's Prius.

He saw the house number, but the car parked in front wasn't the one he associated with Diane. It was a Ford F-150 pickup—probably a couple of years old. Had Diane traded cars? No, he couldn't envision her in a pickup. It most likely belonged to some other visitor.

Joe opened the door of his car but before he could get out, a man exited from the house. It was Martin Perry. Joe didn't particularly want to talk with him, especially after what Diane had told him. Nevertheless, Martin had seen him and appeared to be headed that way.

"Dr. Adams," he said, stopping a few feet from Joe. "Making a house call?"

"Looks like it, doesn't it? And what brings you here?"

"Visiting Ina." And with no further explanation, Martin climbed into the pick-up, started it, and drove away.

Wilma answered the door, the dachshund at her heels. "Oh, Dr. Adams. Come in—but don't let Bruce out. He's been a little rambunctious since Ina got home from the hospital."

Joe navigated the doorway, careful to keep the little dog from getting through. "Is Ina getting along okay here at home? Are you answering the door because she doesn't feel like it?"

"No, she's feeling fine. I'm just trying to keep her from being too active." She led the way into the living room and pointed to Ina, ensconced in her recliner/rocker with the remote from the TV close at hand.

"Dr. Adams," she said, muting the set but leaving it on. "What brings you here? Did something turn up after I left the hospital? I hope not."

Joe made a palms-down "safe" gesture with both hands. "Everything's fine. I was just in the neighborhood, and thought I'd check on you." He eased into a chair. "It looks like you're doing okay, and Wilma is taking good care of you."

Ina looked around and her face seemed to brighten at the realization that she was at home. "I'm doing fine. I've tried to get Wilma to leave, but she wants to stay here tonight."

Joe nodded. Now seemed as good a time as any to bring up the question that had been at the back of his mind since seeing the F-150 parked outside. "Didn't I see Martin Perry leave here as I was coming up?"

"Yes. He dropped by to see me, make sure I didn't need anything. And he told me that he'd be certain a police car would come by several times tonight."

"He seems to be taking good care of you,"

"Though he's not my son-in-law, Martin's been very nice to me—even if it didn't work out between him and Diane." She lowered her voice for the next part. "Martin said he tried to visit with me in the hospital, but he got a call that tied him up. He works so hard—as hard as you do, sometimes."

Joe waited a few seconds, but apparently that was the extent of the information Ina wanted to pass on about Martin. "So, Diane isn't around?" Joe asked, casually.

Ina adjusted the quilt that covered her legs. "No, I decided that there was no reason for her to be here. Wilma and Bruce would take care of me."

"Bruce? Oh, the dog." *The one that almost tripped me up at the door.*

"Sorry you missed Diane, but you'll see her around the hospital tomorrow. I guess that's soon enough."

Time for Joe to make it clear that he'd come—at least, ostensibly—to see his patient. "Ina, you're the one I wanted to see. And you're feeling okay?"

"Oh, yes. Wilma's here, Diane told me to call if I need her, and Martin—well, he just left. I've got lots of people taking care of me." Ina leaned toward Joe and lowered her voice a bit. "I've never really had a chance to ask you. Did things go well on the date you had with my daughter? I was hoping that she was on her way to getting her life together and moving on."

Joe wondered how she got her information. Nothing to be gained by asking, though. "I think it went very well. I don't know about Diane, but I think she enjoyed it as well. We haven't really had a chance to talk about it further since your ... your heart attack." He hated to use those words, but most people understood them, although nowadays most patients lived a fairly normal life after one.

"Well, I hope you'll talk about it soon. She's put her life on hold long enough. I want her to ... That is, I hope that she ..." She took a deep breath. "I think it's time for her to have a life of her own."

Well, there's an answer to the question that's been foremost in my mind. Now to communicate it to Diane.

...

Diane intended to call her mother right after supper that night. However, she fell asleep in front of the TV, and when she woke it was late. Oh, well. If Ina needed anything, she would call. Besides, Diane had practically lived in her mother's hospital room for the past day and a half. She was due some quiet time. After a quick shower, Diane fell into bed and essentially passed out.

The next morning, she was still sleepy, and because she slept through her alarm, Diane had to make do with a quick phone call to her mother. She made this from her car on the way to work. Since she was in a hurry, the conversation didn't last long, but she came away with the impression that her mother was the same old Ina she'd been for years.

Once she arrived at the hospital, Diane was swept into the routine of the emergency room. When she had a lunch break, she headed for the cafeteria, where she saw Joe sitting by himself at a table in the corner.

"Mind if I join you?" she asked.

"Oh, please do. I'd intended to call you if we hadn't run into each other."

"I know. We were going to talk about our next date, but we were ..." She searched for a word. "I guess we were short-circuited." She put down her tray, unloaded the salad and iced tea, then took a chair across the table from him. "Are you about through with your meal?"

Joe shoved his empty soup bowl away in answer. "Yes, but that doesn't mean we can't have a conversation. Let me talk while you eat. Then, after you've eaten a bit, it will be your turn."

After Diane nodded and began to work on her salad, Joe said, "Your mother is doing fine after the heart problem she had. Do you want to talk about us, now?"

She put down her fork and addressed Joe. "Well, mother's heart status made me think about how much she depended on me."

"No, I don't think that's true!" Joe reached for his iced tea glass but found it empty. "I think you've used her to keep from moving out of your comfort zone." He held up his hands to stop what appeared to be a rejoinder. "Oh, I don't think you did it consciously. You didn't want to go out because of your past, and you used your relationship with your mother as an excuse. I finally broke through your reticence, and what was keeping you turned out to be more of a problem to you than to me. At this point, I think you need to get past that other hurdle, the one you've put in your own way. It's time you moved past taking care of your mother."

"Joe, that's not true."

He shook his head. "Actually, I talked with Ina last night and found out that she was happy you'd gone out with me. She hoped you'd move on ... and so do I."

"You talked with her about this?"

"I came by her house late yesterday. She said she was glad you'd gone out with me. She tried to be circumspect, but what she wanted to know was whether I intended to carry it forward."

Diane leaned a bit closer. "And?"

"I said it depended on you." Joe shoved his chair back and stood. "So, I guess the ball's in your court. Are you going to continue using her for an excuse, or move on with a life of your own?"

...

Joe's words continued to tickle at the back of Diane's mind. The ball truly was in her court now, and she wanted to return the serve, yet she was unsure. About Joe? No. She'd asked Julie about him and gotten a positive answer. The recommendation given him by Dr. Carpenter was an unqualified yes. And her time with him had left her with no doubts that moving ahead with Joe was the right thing. So why was she finding it difficult to pull the trigger?

Had her hesitancy to date again have to do with a sense of dirtiness that stemmed from what Martin had done? Was it related to the debt she felt she owed her mother? Or was Joe right? Were these just her defense mechanisms to keep everything the way it was?

After she was at home that afternoon, she kicked off her shoes, relaxed in her most comfortable chair, and called Julie. *Oh, let her be home. I should have checked with her the last time I saw her. It—* "Julie. I'm glad you're home."

"Is your mother okay? Did she really have a heart attack this time?"

"She's doing fine—no different than she was before the heart problem."

Julie's sigh came clearly over the phone. "I'm glad. You've had your share of trouble."

"And the most recent heart attack came right after my date with Joe Adams, which is why I didn't call you to tell you about it." She took a deep breath. "But that brings up a decision I need to make, now that I've been assured that my mother is doing okay."

"And that is?

"A second date."

"With Joe Adams?" The reply came so rapidly that Julie was either very certain or had thought about it ahead of time. "That's a no-brainer. Go for it."

Julie didn't know the details of the things that were holding her back. But her advice had been good so far. Joe was the only one with whom she'd fully shared her story. She'd unburdened herself, and then what was it he had said? Basically, it boiled down to her shame being between her and God—and He'd already forgotten it.

"I guess there's no harm in one more date," she said. "We'll just see where it goes from here."

5

"I'm going to be gone for a bit," Joe told his nurse. "One of my patients has shown up in the emergency room. From the sounds of it, I shouldn't be gone long."

"Your next patient cancelled, and I'll tell the ones following her that you've been called away on an emergency," she said.

Joe's office was in the professional building attached to the hospital, an easy walk from one to the other. As he walked, he let his thoughts go to Diane. Was she working in the ER today? Since they'd last seen each other several days ago, he had maintained a "hands-off" policy, with no phone calls between the two.

Today, he was bound to run into her if she were on duty. Undoubtedly, they would converse after his "emergency" was controlled. Should he speak first? And if so, what was he going to say? He was still ready to take their relationship forward. Was Diane ready to do the same?

As Joe entered the hospital and moved to the emergency room, he recalled how he'd hesitated to ask Diane for that first date, and how many things he'd found standing in her way. He'd gotten past so many barriers. Now he'd find out if she was ready to move on.

...

Diane was on duty today, and was assisting the ER doctor, Dr. Carpenter, with Joe's patient. The woman, Mrs. Atkinson, was sure that she had a heart attack. However, both Diane and

Dr. Carpenter, were leaning toward a diagnosis of a gas pocket in the lower esophagus. The woman had a tendency—according to her ER records—to call every little pain in the area just below her breastbone a heart attack. But even though her EKG today showed no abnormalities, Dr. Carpenter decided that her own doctor, because of his familiarity with the past EKGs as well as Mrs. Atkinson's history, should be consulted and make the final decision.

"Meanwhile, let's give her a pink lady. I'll bet she's symptom-free by the time Dr. Adams gets here," Dr. Carpenter said.

Pink lady was the name given the cocktail sometimes used to quickly diagnose gastrointestinal complaints. The ingredients were an antacid together with an antispasmodic, sometimes with a topical anesthetic added, and in this case, they worked wonders in relieving the patient's symptoms.

When Dr. Adams entered the ER, Dr. Carpenter filled him in on the patient's problem. Confirmation of the history and exam didn't take long, and Dr. Adams saw no change in her EKG from all the ones done in the past.

"I agree with you. I think she's having cardiospasm." he said to Dr. Carpenter. By this, he didn't mean her symptoms were of cardiac origin, but rather were due to spasm of the cardiac sphincter of the esophagus. "She's had it before, and it usually is better by the time she sees me. But better safe than sorry, though," Dr. Adams said. "Even though her EKG is within normal limits, I'll give her the cardiac warnings as well."

He spent some time going over his findings, and Diane noticed the woman nodding in agreement as the doctor spoke. Her pain having resolved by this time, she promised to follow-up with Dr. Adams in a week, with avoidance of triggering foods as well as a trial on a new acid blocker.

"But don't hesitate to call me before then if you have questions or need to be seen earlier."

There were no other patients in the emergency room needing attention, so Diane busied herself in cleaning up the cubicle they had just used when she heard a voice behind her. "Let me take you away from all this."

Without turning, she said with a smile, "I've heard that line before."

"Did it ever work?" Joe asked.

"Not yet," she said. "Just a moment." She walked away, said a few words to Dr. Carpenter, then motioned for Joe to follow her into the break room. As she waited in the otherwise empty room, she knew what she was going to do, but wondered if she was making the right decision. Julie had thought so, when they talked last night. Matter of fact, she was delighted when her friend shared the news with her about starting dating again—especially with Joe Adams.

Joe entered the break room and closed the door. He took Diane gently by the shoulders and said, "It's time to make up your mind."

"And you don't have any doubts about moving forward?"

"Of course I do. I wouldn't be human if I didn't. I suspect that you feel the same way too."

Diane had decided that the time had come to move forward—despite what had happened before. Joe wasn't Martin. He was different. "Yes. Just tell me when and where we're going."

. . .

Joe had just finished seeing his last patient of the afternoon when his nurse caught him coming out of the exam room and pulled him aside.

"Mr. Swanson is in the waiting room. He doesn't have an appointment. Says it's not a medical problem, but he really needs to see you."

Bill Swanson had just lost his wife to cancer after what could best be described as a hard battle, both on her part and his. At first, Joe was tempted to send him on his way, but as he thought about it, he felt he could at least offer some help to the man, maybe assist him in finding a grief group or put him in touch with people who could offer some support. "Bring him in," Joe said.

Swanson was older than Joe by perhaps 30 years, and his circumstances recently had made him appear even older. Today he wore work pants and a shirt that were clean but a bit wrinkled as though they had never seen an iron. He was clean shaven but had missed several spots. Although his wife had been buried more than two weeks earlier, his eyes were red-rimmed.

Joe directed Swanson to one of the two chairs opposite the desk, then took the second one himself and turned it so that the two men were essentially facing each other. He didn't want any artificial barrier such as his desk between them. "I'm sorry for your loss," he began.

Swanson shook his head. "I just don't know what to do. Maybe I need some pills or something. I can't seem to get over her death."

"Pills can help, but antidepressants can only do so much." Joe knew from his own experience that human touch was invaluable, so he touched the man. "As you may know, I underwent a similar situation some time ago when my wife, Gloria, passed away. And I know from my own experience that the first few weeks, few months, perhaps longer are difficult times. We think we're getting past it, and then some trigger or other hits us and we find ourselves crying and in the depths of depression again."

"That's exactly how I feel," Swanson said. "It's sort of one step forward, two backwards. I really have only a partial recollection of the time of the funeral. It's sort of like I was walking through a haze."

"We're told that men don't cry, but that's not true. Don't become a victim to that. Cry when you need to." He paused. "Do you have others who you can call on?"

Swanson shook his head. "I had my son and daughter-in-law around for a time after my wife died, but they left. Now that they're gone, I just move around the house aimlessly."

"I know. It's hard to find things to occupy your time or the will to do them," Joe said. "But let me point you toward some things I found helpful. And believe it or not, things are going to get better—little by little."

"I ... I don't know if I can accept that."

"I know. But it's true."

Swanson shook his head. "I sometimes think it would be better if we'd both died together." He reached into his pants pocket and brought out a revolver.

...

Diane steered her little Prius toward her mother's home. She wanted to tell Ina about her dates with Joe Adams—the first one and the next one. But she figured that she should deliver this development to her mother in person, not via a phone call.

Although Ina—according to Joe—would be happy with Diane's decision, she wasn't totally sure that was accurate. There was a difference in saying her mother would welcome the fact that her daughter would be dating and the actuality of living with those changes. How would she react when she no longer had Diane for errands? Would Wilma be enough?

She dug her cell phone from her purse and when she was stopped for a traffic light, entered the number for Joe's office. When Joe's receptionist answered, she identified herself and asked to speak to him if he were free.

"He's seeing his last patient of the day. It shouldn't be—"

Her sentence was cut off by the sound of a shot, followed by a scream.

...

Joe had faced guns in the hands of patients on a couple of occasions. Things had turned out okay both times, but each situation was different. He hoped he could defuse this one without it ending in bloodshed.

"Bill, what's the gun for?" Joe asked.

Bill Swanson didn't reply. Neither did he give Joe the gun.

The doctor leaned toward his patient and began to speak quietly but earnestly. His words were directed toward Swanson, but his eyes were focused on the gun, which was slowly coming from its resting place in the patient's lap upward to point toward Joe.

The man moved his finger from the trigger guard to rest on the trigger itself. The bullets in the chamber glinted in the light from the fluorescent fixture, benign at rest but ready to be agents of death with just a slight increase in pressure by the index finger.

One more try. "Bill, give me the gun. You don't want to hurt either one of us. That's not going to help."

Swanson merely shook his head but didn't speak.

"Are you feeling like you have nothing further to live for?" Joe asked. "I know the feeling. But you're not alone. Didn't you say something about a son?"

It seemed like an eternity before Swanson replied. "He's never been close. And he's got his own family now. Now that his mother is gone, I doubt that I'll see him even as often as I did before."

As the man spoke, Joe watched the revolver continue to move upward. Now it pointed at Swanson's own head. It was apparent to Joe that his patient wanted to take his own life. He couldn't let that happen.

"One last time. Give me the gun."

Joe tried to think of what he'd read about what to do when facing a revolver. Put the web of his hand under the hammer to prevent it from striking the cartridge? Grab the cylinder to prevent it turning? And if he were unsuccessful, what then?

Meanwhile, Swanson said, "No. It's just better if I do this."

Joe realized that there was no time left. No time for talk. No words that might help. If he were going to act, it had to be now.

His hand darted out just before Swanson pulled the trigger. The noise the gun produced was deafening. A flash from the barrel end came simultaneous with the shot, and then everything was quiet.

...

"What's going on?" Diane's words got no reply. Instead, what she heard, along with the woman's scream, was the phone dropping on the desk. The best way to find out what was happening was to go to Joe's office, and she realized that she wanted to find out. More than that, she wanted Joe to be all right. She turned the car around and headed there as quickly as she could.

When she arrived, a policeman was talking with Joe's receptionist and nurse. There was a mobile ICU idling outside, but she didn't see the paramedics. They must be inside.

Diane was both anxious to go to Joe and apprehensive about what she might see. She steeled herself and slipped by the policeman and the staff, who were still in earnest conversation in the waiting room. She cautiously peered through the partially opened door to Joe's office.

The first thing she saw was Joe, sitting in one of the chairs across from his desk, blood on his face—only a small amount, but just seeing blood on Joe's face was enough to shock her. An attendant from the ambulance crew was bent over him, using a wet cloth to clean off the blood. By Joe stood another policeman, holding an evidence bag with a revolver in it.

Joe looked up and saw Diane. "What are you doing here?"

"I called your office and asked for you. Before your receptionist could say anything, I heard a shot. I turned my car around to come here. Are you all right? What happened?"

Joe held up his hand to indicate she should wait. The man in the other chair was coming to his feet and climbing onto the collapsible stretcher. "Do I need to ride with you?" he asked him.

"I ... I'll be okay. They say they just want to check me at the emergency room." The man took a ragged breath. "I want to thank you for keeping me from making a big mistake. All I got was a scalp wound, but it could have been permanent."

Joe turned back to Diane. "Mr. Swanson has been depressed since his wife died. While I was counseling him, he tried to commit suicide. I managed to deflect the pistol just as it fired. He got by with just a graze, but you know how wounds of the scalp bleed."

"And you?"

"I'm okay—just a little shaken up by all this."

She had a dozen questions, but Joe didn't seem ready for them. That was okay. Her talk with her mother could wait. Plans for the future could wait. Nothing was important right now except that Joe was all right, and it came as a surprise to Diane that the incident had elicited such strong feelings in her. Maybe she cared for Joe—maybe a lot.

. . .

The attempted suicide in Joe's office had taken place on a Wednesday afternoon. Diane decided not to mention the incident to her mother. She indicated to her in passing that she was going on a second date with Joe Adams, and let it go at that.

Joe picked her up on Saturday night and they went to the same restaurant as before. In the car, he said, "I do know other places. It's just that I like this one."

"I do, too," said Diane.

They filled the ride with small talk, none of it forced. Diane didn't tell Joe that when she heard the gunshot a few days earlier and rushed to his office, she realized that her feelings toward him were deeper than any she had ever felt—even with Martin. That had been infatuation. This was . . . Dare she say it? This was beginning to look like the real thing.

Nothing was ever said about it, but she got the impression that Joe experienced those feelings as well.

Inside, they were shown to the same table as previously. "Have you recovered from the incident at your office?" Diane said, after they had been seated and the menus placed in front of them.

"Pretty much," said Joe. "Mr. Swanson's wound to his head wasn't serious. It will heal without a scar. Unfortunately, the same can't be said about the damage to his psyche. He'll need quite a bit of counseling before he gets past his attempt to take his own life."

"Is he going to require a lot of therapy?"

"More than I can give him," Joe said. "But he's going to see a good psychiatrist. And I'm going to be available to him if he wants to see me."

The waiter came to take their drink orders and shortly after that, they ordered their food.

The evening progressed with no dearth of topics. Finally, after the plates had been cleared and they were enjoying coffee, Joe said, "Is there going to be a third date?"

There was no hesitation in Diane's reply. "That's up to you, this time. I'll be ready."

The Saturday night date gave rise to another and another. Soon, they settled into a routine of having dinner together each Saturday evening. They also began to see each other between dates, sometimes inadvertently, sometimes on purpose.

After a half-dozen such dates, Joe said, "This is awkward, but I think what we're doing is what the kids call 'going steady.'"

Diane thought a bit. "We might use a bit more adult language, I imagine. But yes—that's our status right now." *And it could become something more.*

In the car after their dinner, Diane asked, "Joe, would you mind very much if we go by Mother's house tonight?"

"No problem," he said. "Do you want to tell her about us?"

"I think she already suspects. No, I think that, ever since she came home from the hospital, she's been getting just a little weaker. If you agree, maybe you can talk to her about coming in for a checkup. She doesn't respond to me as well as she used to."

"I'll see what I can do," he said.

"You don't think it's too late tonight to visit her?"

Joe looked at the clock on the dash. "We got through eating fairly early. And I don't think your mother is asleep now." He parked in front of Ina's house. "Besides, if the lights are off, we can drive on by."

The question became moot, when they noticed all the lights on and the sound of the TV coming through the closed door. At a nod from Diane, Joe knocked on the door—at first gently, then more forcefully.

"Maybe she's asleep in front of the TV set," Diane said. She rummaged in her purse and found her keys. "I've had this key for a long time, but usually when I come over the door is unlocked. Let's see if I need the key."

She turned the knob and found that the door was locked. "Well, glad she locked up after dark." Diane opened the door with her key and called, "Yoo-hoo. Anybody awake?"

Ina was seated in her recliner facing the TV set, which was going full blast. "Sound asleep," Diane said as she stepped around in front of her mother. She shook her, gently at first, then more vigorously. She put her hand in front of her mother's mouth and nose, feeling for exhalations. Then she put one hand on Ina's neck, looking for a pulse. After a long moment, she turned to Joe, who had followed her in.

No screaming. No hysterics. Just saying in a sad, low voice, "Oh, Mother."

. . .

Joe did all the things he knew to do, all of which confirmed that Ina Macklin was beyond his ability to help. He didn't have any of his equipment, instruments, or medications available, but it didn't matter. She was dead.

Nevertheless, he palpated for the carotid pulse in the neck and felt none. Lacking a stethoscope, he put his ear against her chest but heard no heartbeat. After he checked her pupils and found that they were fixed and dilated, he turned to Diane and slowly shook his head.

"I know," she said. "I sort of knew it when I saw her sitting in the recliner—not rocking, as she always did, but unmoving."

"I'd guess it was a heart problem of some sort, knowing her history. It looks like she probably went very quickly." He wasn't sure whether Diane wanted more information but answered her unspoken question anyway. "Although she died without a doctor in attendance, I can certify her death as cardiac failure. An autopsy won't be legally necessary."

Diane shook her head vigorously. "No! There should be an autopsy—a complete one."

6

Diane only had a few calls to make. Her sister, Patricia, of course was the first one, and— as anticipated—the most difficult. Herbert answered the phone, but as soon as he heard the news, he passed the phone off to Patricia.

The stunned silence that followed Diane's announcement was broken by her sister almost wailing. "But she was doing so well."

"Joe thinks it was sudden, so she didn't feel any pain. But I've seen her just about every day, and she's been getting progressively weaker," Diane said. She moved on to the next thing on her list. "Do you want me to choose the funeral home?"

The prolonged silence that followed was broken by words partially muted, probably by her sister's hand over the receiver as Patricia relayed the news to her husband. Finally, Patricia said, "Sure. Choose the funeral home. And I guess the services will be at the church Mother attended."

More mumbled words in the background, then Patricia said, "Diane, with her history, will there have to be an autopsy? Joe can sign the death out as some kind of cardiac event, can't he?"

Diane knew this was coming. "In Texas, there's a stipulation that the coroner can omit an autopsy if the person was under the care of a physician for the condition that possibly killed them." She hurried on. "But it might be weird if Joe signed the death certificate. Personally, I think there should be an autopsy. Joe said he'd arrange it."

"Mom didn't have any siblings, and Dad died several years ago. Isn't it up to the oldest child to give permission?" Patricia asked.

You've always let me handle all the other things that required time and effort. Why are you starting now? "Actually, there's no need for permission in this case. There's a question—at least, in my mind— of whether her death was natural."

"I don't understand."

"If she died a natural death, that's something that, with time, we could eventually accept. But there's a possibility that her death wasn't natural."

"And if it wasn't?"

"Then we need to know who murdered her ... and why."

At that, Patricia stopped arguing and Diane heaved a sigh of relief. It was hard enough to cope with her mother's death. It was almost too much to have to convince her sister that an autopsy was a good thing. But she knew in her heart that it was necessary.

. . .

Ina died on Saturday. The days passed quickly before her funeral, and where possible Patricia get the input of her older sister on every decision. There was no body at the funeral, of course. That would be released after the toxicology report was received. At that point, a private burial would follow. This was simply a celebration of Ina Macklin's life.

Diane looked around to see those gathered at the First Congregational Church for the service, and was surprised to an extent at the turn-out. Then she directed her attention to those sitting in the first row, the seats occupied by the "family." At the extreme end of the first row, separated from the others by a couple of vacant seats, was Wilma Fairbanks, twisting a handkerchief and sniffling intermittently. She had demonstrated real grief upon learning of Ina's death— probably even more than a member of the family. Then again, Diane had sometimes wondered if Wilma and the dog, Bruce, weren't really her mother's true family.

Next to her was Martin Perry, also separated from the family by empty seats. For this occasion, he was dressed in a conservative dark blue suit and white shirt. He, too, had demonstrated real sorrow at Mrs. Macklin's death. Although he had shown his true colors to her youngest daughter, Martin had remained a friend to Ina, at least, judging by his actions and the frequency of his visits.

In the middle of the front row, as befitted her status as eldest daughter, Patrica sat next to her husband, Herbert. She wore a deep blue, almost black dress, accented by a single strand of pearls. He was outfitted in what Diane always thought of as his "lawyer clothes": dark gray pinstripe suit, white shirt, conservative tie.

Seated next to Herbert and Patricia was Diane. To her left sat Joe Adams. She had just naturally included him in the family group, although he wasn't really one of them.

. Diane was certain that Patricia and Herbert were already calculating their share of their mother's estate. Surely the same thing wouldn't be true of Joe. His actions had always been honorable—but then, so had Martin's until . . .

The pastor continued to say things that Diane knew would be lost from everyone's minds before the conclusion of the service. What he said would be quickly forgotten. What would be real was the hole Ina's passing would leave in each life represented there. That would become more real as time went on. For now, she concentrated on just getting through it all.

. . .

Diane came out the ER door at the end of her shift, her first one back after her mother's death, and practically ran into Joe.

"I presume you have some information that won't wait," he said.

"I wanted your evaluation. The police sent me a copy of the autopsy findings—I guess Patricia got one too. But some of the things were beyond me, and I thought you might help me interpret them." She pointed in the general direction of the lobby. "Why not find a relatively quiet place to sit while you go over them?"

She led Joe to the lobby of the hospital, where she indicated two seats far from anyone else. Diane pulled a large sheaf of paper from her purse and handed it to Joe, who studied it in silence for perhaps five minutes.

"The autopsy on Ina's body revealed no evidence of foul play," he said.

"But the tox screen isn't back?" she asked.

"No, that takes a while longer."

"Then why did the police call me today and say that her cause of death was most likely a homicide, even with a negative autopsy and before the toxicology screen is returned?" she said.

Joe looked down at the sheets in his hand. "The autopsy showed that the stents were working. There was no enlargement of the heart, nothing to suggest any more cardiac disease than would be found in someone of your mother's age. The preliminary interpretation was probable cardiac arrhythmia, because there was no overt evidence of anything to prove otherwise. But you're right—the cause of death shows as 'pending police investigation.'"

"So, the police—and I wish now I had written down the name of the man who called me—the police will be going through the house looking for more clues?"

"Yes, and if I were you, if there's anything you need to get from your mother's house, I'd suggest you get it now."

. . .

Diane was surprised when she decided later that afternoon to take Joe's advice. Her mother's house had apparently already been declared a crime scene. Yellow tape blocked the entrance to the house, and although it was easy enough to duck under the chest-high barrier, it was difficult to get past the patrolman standing guard at the door with a clipboard.

"I'm her daughter, Diane Macklin. I just want to see if there's anything personal in there. I'm not trying to cover up anything. Actually, I have an alibi for the time involved."

"I'm sorry, ma'am," he replied. "The sergeant will want to talk to you, but right now he and some patrolmen are going through the house, gathering evidence. Would you like to wait for him to finish?"

Before Diane could reply, she heard another voice, this one coming from a man in uniform who walked up behind the officer guarding the door. "Did I hear you identify yourself as Diane Macklin?" he asked.

The new officer had three chevrons on his sleeve. This must be the sergeant referred to by the guardian blocking her way. "That's right," she said. "And you are?"

"Sergeant Hathaway. And you have the sympathy of our entire department at your loss." He stepped past the patrolman with the clipboard and continued the conversation on the porch. "I'm sorry to keep you out of the house, but we'll finish gathering evidence today. By tomorrow, you and your sister should be able to get in."

Has Patricia been here poking around? "You haven't seen my sister today?"

"Called her this afternoon to tell her about the autopsy report. She's coming by the station to give me a statement tomorrow morning. You haven't gotten my voicemail, evidently, but I'll tell you directly. Would it be convenient for you to come tomorrow afternoon?"

"I get off about mid-afternoon tomorrow," Diane said. "I suppose I can come by after that."

"Fine. Just ask at the desk for me—Sergeant Hathaway—and they'll get me."

"I was surprised when you said that the tox screen wasn't back yet but you're already investigating this as a murder."

"I shouldn't have let that out. But you'll find out all about it in due time," the sergeant said. "Just let us do our jobs for now."

As Diane turned away from the house, her mind was busy. The police were now apparently investigating Ina Macklin's death as a murder. Patricia had already received her call. *I guess he called her first because she's the oldest. Or was she under suspicion?*

As predicted by Joe, the police had lost no time in starting their investigation. Sergeant Hathaway seemed all right, so far. She wondered if Martin were involved in some fashion. Since he'd only recently made corporal, she guessed seniority had something to do with it.

Maybe she'd know more after she gave her statement tomorrow.

A homicide that doesn't show up on autopsy or toxicology. That's a mystery.

. . .

Later that evening, Joe frowned and rearranged his posture on Diane's couch. "Are you sure this will just be routine? I can go with you tomorrow if it would help. Do you want me to arrange for a lawyer to be there?"

Since Ina Macklin's death Diane had spent many evenings with Joe. They hadn't discussed future plans, but she found herself liking his company, and missing him when he wasn't around. They were "keeping company," as her mother would have said.

She turned slightly and spoke to him. "I realize you've been busy enough with your practice. There's no need for you to disrupt your schedule just to accompany me tomorrow. And I don't see the need for any lawyer."

"Are you satisfied with this guy who's investigating Ina's death?"

She paused and considered the question. "Sergeant Hathaway is new to me, but so far he seems pretty straightforward."

"You never heard of Hathaway before? Didn't—excuse me, if this makes you uncomfortable—but didn't Martin introduce you to a number of the other policemen while you were engaged to him?"

"Oh, a handful, but not to any of the higher ups. And he didn't make corporal himself until very recently. Why should our not knowing Hathaway before this make any difference?" she said.

"I don't know," Joe said. "I guess I'm being a bit paranoid, but anything the police are involved with makes me suspicious."

"Is it because of my past relationship with Martin? I've told you—"

Joe nodded. "Oh, somewhere in my subconscious, I guess there's a bit of that," he said. "Somehow, I have this little niggling suspicion that Martin will rear his head and figure into this investigation." He moved closer on the couch and put his arm around her. "And I guess I'd feel better if I were with you tomorrow.

"I don't think I have anything to worry about," she said.

. . .

The next afternoon Diane realized that, despite her past relationship with Martin, she had never been to the local police station. However, she found it with no real problem, thanks at least in part to the navigation system on her car. She identified herself to the officer at the front desk and said Sergeant Hathaway was expecting her. Diane waited less than five minutes before Hathaway came to get her.

She expected to be in an interview room such as she'd seen on TV, but instead he led her to a desk in the corner of what she took to be the squad room. Other desks, both empty and occupied, were scattered about, but she was grateful to see that no one was close to the one where she was told to sit. When she was as comfortable as possible, Hathaway pulled a tape recorder from a drawer and placed it between them.

"This tape is just to make sure we don't miss anything you say."

"Will you record this visually as well?"

"We won't use a camera to record your interview," Hathaway said. "And you're not a suspect, so you don't need to be given a Miranda warning."

Diane nodded. *That's reassuring, I guess.*

"All we need is your recollection of events from that night—where you were, what time, what you did. If there are any gaps, I'll ask questions. Okay?"

After she assured him that she understood, Hathaway turned on the recorder, said a few preliminary sentences, then leaned back and motioned for her to go ahead.

Diane was surprised at how rapidly and naturally it flowed, once she got over her initial nervousness. She finally stopped thinking about every sentence and whether it pointed the finger of suspicion at someone, and simply told her story. It didn't take long. "And that's about it," she concluded.

Hathaway opened his eyes—she had been afraid he was sleeping—and said, "Why did you think an autopsy was important? The law in the state of Texas allows—"

"I know. Since she had known heart problems, Joe—that is, Dr. Adams—could have pronounced her and signed the death certificate. But she'd been getting weaker over the past few weeks. I guess I just wanted to be certain."

"And as part of the autopsy, they did a toxicology screen," Hathaway said.

"What did it show?" Diane asked.

"I'm afraid we're not going to release that."

"Not even to me? I'm her daughter."

He shook his head. "Let's just say that the tox screen doesn't hold the answer. It goes back to something we found out about in the course of our investigation."

7

The cafeteria of the hospital was neither more nor less crowded than usual at noon the next day. "I'm glad you could get away for lunch," Joe said to Diane as he unloaded his tray and took a seat.

All around them, people were coming and going, the cafeteria serving its usual mixture of patient families and medical personnel. But the doctors, nurses, technicians, and everyone connected with the medical complex seemed intent on eating and getting back to work, while the patients' families were intent on discussing with one another the interpretation of whatever latest news they were able to glean about their friend or loved one, both glad to be away from their vigil yet anxious to return.

Amidst all this, Diane and Joe were relatively isolated, sitting at table for two, removed from their nearest neighbor by a couple of tables, and around the corner from most of the rest. Both had realized that lunch plans might have to be scrubbed, depending on medical emergencies, but it had all worked out for them to eat together.

"My interview with the sergeant was pretty uneventful," Diane said. "Well, he did let slip something about not needing the tox screen to prove murder. But that's all he would say."

Joe took a bite of his tuna sandwich and washed it down with a healthy swallow of iced tea. Then he said, "I'm sorry we won't have an opportunity to get together this evening, but I have a staff meeting."

Diane took a bite of her salad, chewed, and swallowed. "That's fine. I have some things to do tonight."

"Anyway, I have some more information that may be pertinent as we try to decipher your mother's estate—information I've managed to gather from here and there over the past several days."

"I thought we'd just let Sergeant Hathaway do his job," she said. "Although I wish this were over already."

"It does take time," Joe said. "And the police have to reach a conclusion."

"Because ..."

"Because first of all, no one wants a murderer running loose. And second, don't forget that whoever is responsible for the death can't profit from it—and we're all suspects—so the estate can't be settled yet." He took a small bite from his sandwich, chewed and swallowed. "Meanwhile, as I've said, I have some information that you might find interesting."

"Did you hire a private detective?"

Joe smiled as though he'd drawn a fourth ace. "Better than that. I befriended a particularly curious reporter who's been looking into this."

"How did that come about?"

Joe put his sandwich down and leaned closer. "I took care of her medical problem, and that got me into her good graces. At one point today, we were talking about your mother's passing. She already knew about the will. Then she let slip some of the things she'd found out about the characters in this little scenario."

"Such as ..."

"Your brother-in-law may put up a good front, but if he doesn't start contributing more to the firm's finances, his partners are considering removing him from the group."

"I can't believe it," Diane said. "Patricia hasn't said anything about it."

"Maybe she doesn't know."

Diane took a sip from her iced tea. "What else did you learn?"

"Wilma is barely making it on her Social Security. Her inheritance from Ina is reported to be over 50 thousand dollars. That's a small amount out the total estate, but it would go a long way toward supplementing her income. She certainly needs it—but does she need it badly enough to commit murder?"

"I'm surprised you and I aren't under suspicion."

"Oh, we are," said Joe. "The money from the estate would pay for quite a wedding, as well as giving us a good start in our married life. And rumor has us as good as married already."

"I'm flattered, but—"

"And don't forget that, since I have access to all kinds of medication, I'm implicated."

Diane shook her head. "So, all of us are still suspects."

Joe patted his lips with a paper napkin before putting it atop the remnants of his sandwich. "Wait, there's more. I haven't mentioned the joker in the deck yet. Have you ever wondered why Sergeant Hathaway is taking the lead in this investigation? Not someone, who knows the family well, such as Martin?"

"I just assumed it was because of Hathaway's seniority."

"Maybe. But, according to the reporter, people at the department, mainly the sergeant, have been quietly looking into Martin's activities for some time. It seems that he might be taking things out of the evidence room and selling them ... including drugs."

. . .

The group gathered in the waiting room of the law office the next day talked together in hushed, nervous tones. "I've never been through this before," Diane said.

"None of us have," Joe replied, reaching out to pat her hand. "So, we'll just wait and see what happens."

"I don't know why the lawyer wanted me here," Wilma said from her seat in the corner. She'd automatically separated herself from the group, but in the small waiting area, occupied by only the people waiting to hear from Mr. Gilmore, she didn't have to raise her voice to be heard.

"I'd think that this could have been handled some other way, maybe by phone, without our having to take the time out of our day to come here," Patricia said.

Sitting beside his wife, Herbert held his iPhone in his hand, apparently reading it as he waited. Only the jiggling of his right leg, which was crossed over his left, betrayed his nervousness.

Diane's reverie was interrupted by an announcement from the secretary, who put down the phone and said, "Mr. Gilmore is ready for you. Right through that door."

The group rose and began to go through the door the secretary indicated. Once inside, Diane decided that this lawyer certainly looked different than what she expected. She saw a man not much older than herself who rose from his seat on an overstuffed chair and indicated that the individuals should be seated in the couches and side chairs arranged around his own. His desk was on the other side of the room but was apparently not to be used for this event.

"I'm Ina Macklin's attorney, Jerry Gilmore," he said. "I can probably identify most of you, but to be certain, why don't you introduce yourselves to me."

They did, starting with Diane and Joe.

"I realize why Diane is here, but I don't believe I fully understand your role," the attorney said to Joe.

Joe wasn't sure what his position was either. He was more than boyfriend, less than fiancée. He and Diane had not discussed his status after Ina's death, but he didn't think it had changed. Finally, he simply said, "I'm here for Diane."

When everyone had introduced themselves, the attorney said, "Please relax. The 'reading of the will,' as we've come to think of it from mysteries or TV, is a fallacy. We'll probate the will before a judge after we get the final police report and do an inventory of Ina's assets. The purpose of having you here together is to acquaint you with the financial affairs of Mrs. Macklin. I'm sure you're anxious, to a greater or lesser degree, to know what's ahead for you."

Getting no comments or questions from those gathered together, the lawyer went on. "I drew up her will for Ina about two years ago. Rather than name either of her daughters as executrix, she asked me to act in that capacity. But I assure you that I'll consult with both daughters as necessary."

There was some squirming among the audience, but no interruptions. Gilmore continued, "Ina Macklin was well-fixed from her husband's insurance, and she invested the proceeds wisely."

"And you know this how?" asked Herbert.

"Because I took care of her money for her," said the lawyer. "Her assets now are somewhere a bit more than three quarters of a million dollars. She left a rather significant sum to her friend, Mrs. Fairbanks, the only stipulation being that she care for Bruce, her dog."

At this pronouncement, Wilma started to cry but had nothing to say.

"The residual, after her debts are discharged, will be split equally between her two daughters."

"And was that the reason you called us together? Couldn't this have been covered with a letter or something?" It wasn't clear whether Herbert had a real objection or was just flexing his muscle to prove that he, too, was a lawyer.

"That covers the distribution of her assets," Gilmore said. "But there's one more thing. And this should be of interest to you all."

"What?" Joe said.

"Several months before her death, Mrs. Macklin began to suspect that someone was after her money. Therefore, she told me it was her wish—not legally binding, of course—that the police investigate her death if there were any question of it not being natural." He looked directly around at the assembly. "So, if an autopsy hadn't been requested by the family, one would have been requested by me."

"Why would she do that?" The question came from Wilma but was certainly on everyone's mind.

"There's a significant amount of money at stake," Gilmore replied. "So, I guess she wanted to be sure there was no foul play involved."

There was no reply—but each of them looked around the room, as though to say, "Was it you?"

. . .

Diane had just finished her shift the next day when, as she was gathering her things from her locker, her cell phone rang. She hadn't designated a ring tone for her sister, since she almost never called, and it was a surprise when she saw that the Caller ID indicated that the caller was Patricia.

Let's see—Mother is dead, and Patricia has never called me unless she wanted something. She must want something now. Diane wondered what it was.

Whatever Patricia wanted, Diane wasn't ready to talk to her. Actually, this was neither the time nor the place to talk with her. *Maybe she'll leave a message. Otherwise, I'll call her later. Right now, I'm ready to get out of here.*

Diane let her mind consider the mundane things she had to do while her body got into her car and started it. Soon she looked up and found that she was parked in front of the grocery. Well, perhaps lamb chops and broccoli weren't as exciting as whatever her sister wanted, but their purchase was necessary. She noticed that it was sprinkling, so she grabbed the folding umbrella usually kept in the car.

She did her grocery shopping the same way she did most of her other chores—as fast as possible, already thinking of the next thing on her list. She gathered the bags the checker gave her, added the cash register receipt, and stepped out of the store. The shower had stopped, so she left the umbrella collapsed.

Dianne had put her groceries into the back seat of her hybrid. She fastened her seat belt, started the engine, and just as she was ready to pull away, she was interrupted by the ringing of her phone. She put the car in park, turned off the ignition, and looked at the caller ID on the phone. Diane saw that this time it was Herbert, her brother-in-law calling. Maybe she'd misjudged her sister. Perhaps she'd been in an accident, or some other catastrophe had befallen her.

"Hello."

"Diane, this is Herbert."

"I can see that on my caller ID. What's going on, Herbert."

"Umm, it's important that I see you right now."

Diane thought about it. "Is that why Patricia called me earlier this afternoon?"

"She thought maybe this would be better coming from her sister. But please. It's urgent. There's no time to lose."

"I have to go by my house and get these groceries in the refrigerator. Why don't you come by there?"

"No. We can't seem to be colluding. That's important."

"So, a restaurant is out, too?"

"Yes." There was a prolonged silence before he spoke again. "Why don't you come by our house. It would seem natural that you visit your sister."

Diane didn't know what the secrecy was about. She certainly wasn't afraid to be alone with Herbert, even if Patricia wasn't there. If nothing else, she was probably stronger than him. And if she didn't give in to his choice, this could go on for an hour. "Okay, I'll be there as soon as possible."

It took her only forty minutes before she pulled up at her older sister's house. Herbert's Cadillac was in the circular driveway, and Diane parked her Prius behind it. She was tempted to look over her shoulder as she approached the door. She still didn't understand the need for secrecy, but Herbert had insisted on it.

He answered the door himself and showed her into the living room. Diane looked around and realized that she had been inside this house only a handful of times. She asked, "Is Patricia around?"

"No," Herbert answered. "She's at one of her groups—I'm not sure which one. We're alone here."

Diane noted that her brother-in-law must have come directly from work. He still had his gray pin-striped suit on. He hadn't even taken off his coat. Perhaps he was going back to work after their meeting. Or it was possible that being dressed in the garb of a successful lawyer gave him protective coloration that he needed for the encounter.

"Why should it be secret that we're meeting?" she asked, taking the chair that he indicated.

Herbert sat, then leaned closer to Diane. Although they were alone in the house, he lowered his voice until he was almost whispering. "Because of what I'm about to tell you. I hope this meeting and what comes from it won't get out. You'll see in a minute that it's important."

8

Joe settled himself behind his desk and waited for Diane to choose one of the two chairs across from him. Once she was seated, he asked, "How long before you need to be back in the ER?"

"I've got at least half an hour for my break. Are you good for that long?"

"I have fifteen minutes before my next appointment, but I can stretch this session out further if we need to. I'm surprised that you didn't call me last night after your meeting with Herbert.

"Actually, I thought about calling you, but decided to think about it first—but I still don't have the answer," Diane said.

"Okay, let's see if I can contribute something."

Diane nodded. "I'll boil it down for you, but our meeting lasted over an hour. It apparently was like pulling teeth for Herbert to admit—especially to me—that he was in trouble."

"You mean that perfect Herbert isn't as perfect as we've been led to believe?"

"He needs ten thousand dollars now to get out of the jam that he's in."

Joe brought his chair forward and leaned toward Diane. "That goes along with what I've heard. What did he do?"

"I've always wondered how he and Patricia maintained their lifestyle. Well, apparently it was really important to him—maybe to them both— so when he really needed some money that he didn't have, he took some out of an account belonging to one of his clients and used it. He's done it before, and Ina always bailed him out."

"And now?"

"Now we're coming up again on the time when it will be discovered that he's been dipping into the cash if he doesn't replace the money. And mother can't do it anymore. So, he came to me."

"Well, I'd suggest that we sell your mother's house, but the whole estate is still tied up pending the conclusion of the investigation." Joe doodled on his blotter while he thought. "I guess the simplest thing to do would be to go to the managing partner of his firm, confess what he's done, and throw himself on their mercy. Has he considered that?"

"He rejected that out of hand."

Joe nodded. "I can think of all the bad things they could do if he confessed—removing him from the firm, maybe causing him to lose his law license. But what else can he do? Second mortgage on his – house? Sell that car he's so proud of?"

"He's—what do you call it? He's underwater on the house, mortgaged to the hilt already. The car is leased, and he's two payments behind on it."

Joe stopped doodling on his blotter. He tossed his pen aside. "I certainly don't have the kind of money he needs. Maybe his wife could borrow it against her prospects when your mother's estate is finally settled."

"He had a similar idea, but Patricia would prefer I was the one who approached the lawyer on Herbert's behalf. She wanted me to be the one borrowing against the inheritance."

Joe shook his head. "I don't think it would work. Until the police charge someone with your mother's death, the estate is in limbo. And apparently, all of us—including Herbert— are under suspicion."

Diane got out of the chair and began to pace. "If Herbert doesn't pay off the indebtedness, the consequences might be terrible. He could even go to jail." She stopped her pacing long enough to ask, "Can you think of anything I can do?"

"The only suggestion I have is that he take his medicine. Other than that, I don't have a clue."

As the evening wound down, Diane yawned until Joe finally said, "Okay, I can take a hint. You're had a long day. I'm going home so you can get some rest."

Their good-night kisses had become less like brother and sister and more like a man and woman who truly cared for each other. When all this was over— – Oh, how she wished it were truly over. But until then, Diane didn't feel as though she should make the commitment that she knew was coming.

As she prepared to settle in for the evening, her mind kept coming back to one area, an area surely Sergeant Hathaway and his crew had already looked into. Possibly even found. But what if they hadn't. She'd feel better if she looked herself.

Diane put aside the robe and slippers she had expected to spend the evening in. Instead, she donned jeans, a tee shirt, and loafers worn without socks, all the while telling herself this trip was unnecessary. As something of an afterthought, she not only made sure she had her key to her mother's house but also had a flashlight, in case she decided to keep the lights to a minimum.

Her mother's house was dark, and the crime scene tape had been removed. Diane knew that she had as much right as anyone to go into this house, but nevertheless she felt funny, going into a house she'd entered dozens, no, more like hundreds of times, for this purpose. She'd decided to keep the lights turned off. No use advertising to others that she was there. It was quiet when she opened the door, and Diane was tempted to yell, just to break the silence.

Her mother had kept a desk in what was her bedroom, and that was where she would start her search. It was easy for her to find her way through the gloom until she had exited the "front room," at which point she turned on the flashlight and conducted her search using its beam. A search of all the drawers of the desk didn't yield what she was looking for. Her mother's checkbook was maintained up until the day she died, although the gradual deterioration in her handwriting was apparent. It contained checks written for normal expenses, plus several rather large ones made out to her sister, Patricia. Probably these were the "loans" she would no longer be making. She went back a year in the checkbook and found no payment to an insurance agent or company. Then again, maybe it was one of those policies she'd heard of where you make one large payment when you buy it.

When she'd exhausted her search of the desk and surrounding areas, she looked in the bedroom, but soon decided that was enough. The house was fully dark, except for the beam of her flashlight, and frankly, she wanted to leave. She turned to find her way back to the front room and from there to the front door when she sensed, more than saw, another presence in the room.

"Who's there?" she said.

"Just me." The beam of Diane's flashlight picked out Wilma, standing in the doorway. "I saw a light moving around in this room and decided to investigate."

"Didn't I close the door behind me? And doesn't it lock when I do that?"

"Yes, but I've had a key for years," Wilma said. "I've been keeping an eye on the property until the attorney is ready to settle the estate."

"Yes, I forgot that you had a key."

Diane decided she should explain her presence "I'm looking to see if Mother had an insurance policy. Thus far I haven't found one."

Wilma said, "Maybe that's because Ina gave it to me."

"To you? Why?"

"Because I'm the beneficiary."

. . .

The next day when she had her break, Diane called Sergeant Hathaway. He probably knew about the insurance policy, but just in case he didn't, she'd feel better telling him. She made an appointment to talk with him in person after work that day.

Now, as she sat waiting, she wondered why she'd gone ahead and called the sergeant. She was unsure why she hadn't left it to the sergeant to do his job and simply stayed out of it. That would have been the smarter thing. But then again, as Joe had told her, she didn't always take the best course—just the most direct one.

She had barely seated herself before Hathaway came to get her. "Miss Macklin, let's go into one of the rooms where it's a bit more private," he said.

The room they entered featured a mirror on one wall—probably one-way, she guessed—and was furnished with a table and chairs. As she took a seat and tried to hitch her chair closer, she discovered that it was bolted down. So, this was probably an interrogation room. She hoped it was the only room available. Not that it was going to involve her in a full-fledged interrogation.

"You had something to tell me?" the policeman said. His voice was kindly, his words non-threatening, but nevertheless Diane felt that perhaps she'd done something wrong.

She related her experience of the previous evening, ending with Wilma's revelation that Ina had indeed taken out an insurance policy. "I searched for the policy, then later found out that Wilma had it. She said she gave it to you, but since she was the beneficiary of my mother's policy, I wanted to see if this affected your investigation."

Hathaway leaned back in his chair and exhaled slowly. "True, we've already learned about the insurance policy. And I was a little surprised that Wilma Fairbanks was named the beneficiary. What's more interesting is that it pays double indemnity—forty thousand dollars for accidental death."

Diane whistled silently.

"But Ms. Fairbanks explained it, and it made some degree of sense."

"Well," Diane said, "It doesn't make total sense to me."

The policeman took a sip from the water bottle in front of him. "Your mother wanted to reassure Ms. Fairbanks after an incident that we're investigating."

"What incident?"

Hathaway shrugged. "You don't need to know right now. But I appreciate your telling us about the policy.

. . .

Joe had taken off his shoes after supper. He wiggled his toes and was glad for the feeling of freedom he had developed with Diane. He was also glad that his argyles showed no holes as his feet rested beneath the coffee table. "Are you sure you don't need any help cleaning up?"

"Almost finished. Just relax. I'll join you in a minute."

Usually Diane was talkative throughout dinner, using this time to exchange stories with him about the day's events, but tonight she hadn't seemed to have much to say.

"Oh, you're in your stocking feet," she said as she sat down on the couch beside him. "Did you have a hard day?"

Joe sat forward and started reaching for his shoes, but Diane stopped him. "No, that's all right. I'm glad you feel that much at home."

I'll never have a better chance to bring this up. "I do. And since we're talking about being comfortable with one another, I guess we'd better talk soon about our state of 'going steady.' We both know that this is just a way station on the path to something we know is coming."

"Joe, it will come," Diane said. "But not now."

He opened his mouth, but before he could say anything Diane's phone rang. Joe watched her look at the caller ID with a puzzled expression before answering. The conversation was short—mainly she seemed to be listening. When she ended the call, she turned to Joe and said, "That was Sergeant Hathaway. They'd like to meet with all of us within the next few days."

...

It was a couple of days before everyone could be assembled, but knowing the time of the assembly far enough ahead, she and Joe had been able to arrange their schedules to allow for their attendance.

When she entered, Diane noticed that this was a different room in the police station than the ones she'd seen before. It was basically empty except for the horseshoe of the chairs placed for them, plus the one facing them, which was apparently for Sergeant Hathaway.

She looked around the room at those assembled. Patricia was there, of course, together with her husband, Herbert, sitting to the left of center. She looked a bit pale, but otherwise neither demonstrated any emotion. Wilma Fairbanks had separated herself, perhaps by design, and was sitting at one end of the horseshoe all alone. She was twisting the ever-present handkerchief and her feet were in constant motion. Diane and Joe Adams were seated beside each other in the center of the arrangement of chairs.

In the opposite corner of the group was Martin Perry, occupying himself by looking at his iPhone. Being in the police station was more or less normal for him, so she assumed it was not unusual that he showed no outward signs of apprehension. Diane wondered why her ex-fiancé had been included in the group Sergeant Hathaway had called together.

"I'm getting used to being in the station, but I've never been in this room before," Diane whispered to Joe.

"I'd imagine they don't use it much."

She was about to say something more when Sergeant Hathaway entered the room and took a seat facing the group. "I'll avoid the 'I suppose you're wondering why I've asked you here' speech," he said. "We've concluded our investigation, passed on our findings to the insurance company and Mrs. Macklin's attorney, and you'll hear from them shortly regarding the distribution of her estate."

Diane nudged Joe but didn't say anything.

"Meanwhile, we've found that she was killed by a means that is almost beyond detection. Notice that I said 'almost.'" He looked around the assembled group. "That, of course, means that whoever caused her death can't benefit from her estate."

The silence that followed was broken by Diane's voice. "So, who did it?"

Before he could reply, another policeman entered the room and engaged Hathaway in earnest whispers. She couldn't hear what their discussion was about, but whatever it was, it was going to postpone the sergeant's announcement for another few minutes.

9

In the silence that followed, Diane looked around the room until her gaze lit on her brother-in-law, Herbert. She hadn't heard anything further about his situation since he had told her of his predicament. The man certainly showed no signs of nervousness. Had the law firm reached some sort of settlement with their "black sheep?" And maybe he hadn't killed Ina Macklin, either. If the estate was about to be settled, perhaps he was home free. Just take the money from his wife's share of the estate. Perhaps.

Next to Herbert, Patricia reached out to hold her husband's hand. This wasn't particularly of note, given the circumstances, except that Diane couldn't recall her making a similar gesture in all the time Patricia had been married. She wondered who was being supportive and who was offering support. Surely her sister wasn't so anxious to get her hands on her mother's money that she killed her. Surely not.

Far to one side sat Wilma Fairbanks. She held a lace handkerchief that she was twisting like she was doing battle with it. Could she be nervous because her guilt was about to be revealed? Or was the occasion and setting enough to produce that amount of anxiety in the woman as she remembered the death of her friend?

Diane sneaked a glance at Martin Perry at the same time that the policeman was looking in her direction, so that their eyes met for in instant. Outwardly, Martin seemed unconcerned, almost bored. Diane wondered if that was merely a façade.

He wasn't considered a member of the family, so she wondered once more what he was doing here. If one was to believe the rumors circulating around the police station, maybe Sergeant Hathaway had confirmed that he'd been selling drugs out of the evidence locker. Was it beyond belief that perhaps he had found some means of killing her that might not show up?

Joe was to her immediate left, sitting quietly. He hadn't been cleared—none of them had—but why would he kill Ina Macklin? Was money from her estate important enough that he'd arrange for her death and a subsequent marriage to her younger daughter?

Their whispered conversation over, the other policeman left the room as silently as he'd entered. Sergeant Hathaway looked around to see if he still had the attention of everyone. He had. After all, he was about to reveal the identity of the person who'd been responsible for the death of Ina Macklin.

"One more piece of business before I name the killer," he said. "I presume that you all have heard that I was investigating one of our policemen for selling material from the evidence locker. It's true that such an investigation took place, and while the details of how it worked need not concern you, I wanted to say to each of you that the patrolman in question has been cleared of all charges."

Diane turned to look at Martin. "Then why is he here?" She intended her question to be voiced under her breath, but in the silence that followed Sergeant Hathaway's announcement, it was heard clearly by the entire group.

"No need to be embarrassed, Diane," Martin said. "It made sense that perhaps I had the idea that Mrs. Macklin was somehow standing in the way of my getting together with you again. But it was clear to me as I visited with her that she was thrilled that you had found Joe and were about to make him a part of your life. So, my time with her was only as a friend."

"And your presence here?" Diane asked.

Hathaway answered that one. "It seemed to me that everyone here, to a greater or lesser extent, had suspected Martin of being the killer. So, it was easiest just to announce it to you all at this time."

Diane was still digesting this bit of information when Joe spoke up, directing his question to Sergeant Hathaway. "So, was his presence here just to let us know that your investigation had cleared him?"

"Not at all. I thought it appropriate, given his relation to the decedent, that he be the officer to make the arrest."

"Arrest?" Diane exclaimed.

"Yes. Corporal Perry, please take into custody Mrs. Wilma Fairbanks and charge her with the murder of Ina Macklin."

Martin came around behind the semicircle of chairs, said a few words in Wilma's ear, and then led her away. She said nothing to proclaim her innocence during the encounter. If Diane was reading her right, she seemed to expect what transpired.

The silence that came after that revelation was followed by the buzz of questions. Hathaway held up his hand for silence. "Here's what happened. It goes back to the first time Ina Macklin went to the ER. Records indicate a slow heartbeat and a potassium level that was slightly elevated. As it turns out, this was probably due to a 'tea' that Wilma Fairbanks was giving her. A tea made from oleander leaves.

"We think that she, like many of her generation, learned to treat various complaints, including cardiac ones, with such a tea. Her mother, and probably her grandmother before her, had placed great stock in this oleander tea. And whether by accident or design, she gave her friend more and more oleander tea recently, treating her with higher and higher doses of it until it caused her last cardiac rhythm disturbance—a disturbance that proved fatal."

Diane's voice was raised. "I remember her having oleander growing in her back yard. That must have been where she got it."

Hathaway nodded. "We have a patrolman who's an amateur botanist. He was in the search party with me at Ina's house, and he commented on an oleander stem with leaves still attached that

Mrs. Fairbanks apparently left in the trash there. We looked up the effects of oleander tea, and matched it with the slow heartbeat and elevated potassium on the ER record at her first visit. I began backtracking things. An elevated potassium blood level was present when we looked for it in the blood sample taken for tox screening, and it all began to come together."

"So that's what you meant when you told me the toxicology screen wasn't significant," Diane said.

"Her tox screen was negative. It was increasing doses of oleander tea that drove her potassium up to lethal levels."

. . .

Joe helped Diane into his car, then went around and got behind the wheel, but he didn't start the engine yet.

She kept her eyes straight ahead as she spoke. "I guess we'll hear from Mr. Gilmore about probating the estate, now that we know that Wilma won't profit from mother's death."

"There'll be some back-and-forth about whether her share is held in escrow until after the trial, but that won't affect you," Joe said.

"Do you think Wilma did it on purpose? Was she trying to kill my mother ... or help her get well?"

"The district attorney and eventually the courts will decide that."

"What about Herbert? Sergeant Hathaway didn't mention him," Diane said.

"He's probably going to have to confess to his firm. What the partners there will do, I don't know." Joe waited, still not turning on the ignition. "Are you ready ..."

"No," she said. She turned to him. "I'm not ready yet to take the next step in our relationship. I know where it's going, and I think I'll be fine when it gets there. But, I have a feeling there's something more around the corner. Somehow I'm waiting for the other shoe to drop."

Joe was silent, but when he thought about it, he realized that Diane was right. It was too soon. They should wait for the other shoe to drop.

. . .

More than a week had passed since the police had arrested Wilma for the death of Ina Macklin, and Diane was taking advantage of her day off when the phone rang. She looked at the caller ID and discovered that the call was from her mother's attorney.

Because no one else was available for the job, Bruce, the rescue dog, had needed a home and Diane had volunteered. He skittered around her feet. *Maybe he thinks the phone call is for him.*

She got Bruce calmed down before she answered the phone, then listened as Mr. Gilmore explained to her that the insurance company had agreed that the proceeds of the insurance policy would be put in escrow until Wilma's court case was settled. The same would be done with her share of the proceeds of the estate. This having been settled, he'd be proceeding with probating the document and distributing the assets. She'd hear from his office again with further details.

When she was asked if she had any questions, she said, "No, it sounds like you've got things well in hand. I'll just let you continue to handle the mechanics of the situation." Just then, Bruce capered around her feet. "Meanwhile, Bruce is reminding me that it's time for his mid-morning treat."

When Diane ended the call, she gave Bruce a cookie, then let him into the back yard to do his business. She sat in her favorite chair for a moment, thinking about the events surrounding her mother's death.

Martin had come out of everything as nothing more than an innocent person. Maybe he really had changed.

Wilma's share of the estate was relatively small in comparison with the total amount involved. And maybe it would eventually be decided that she deserved the proceeds of the insurance policy. Whether double indemnity came into play because Ina was murdered—well, that would hinge in the outcome of the trial, then some more negotiations between the insurance company and Wilma's lawyers.

It appeared that she and Patricia were going to inherit a significant amount of money from her mother's estate. Not that it would affect her plans, of course. She'd rather have her mother alive and well instead of all the money in the world.

She heard the front door open. Diane was certain she'd locked it, but perhaps she'd forgotten. She rose from her chair and saw her sister, Patricia, in the front hallway. Of course, she had a key, but Diane couldn't remember her ever using it. She wondered why she'd come now.

"Patricia, I wasn't expecting you."

Patricia closed the door behind her. She reached into her purse and pulled out a snub-nosed revolver. "I guess we'd better get this over with."

Diane was stunned. She couldn't fathom what was going on. Her sister? Why? She asked the first question that came to her mind. "Where did you get the gun?"

"It was Herbert's. He got it when he first went into practice, but for the past year or more he kept it in the bottom of his sock drawer. He probably will never know it's gone. I'll shoot you, then toss it over a bridge railing somewhere and there'll be nothing to connect it with me. If the police should ask about this gun, I'll look for it, find it gone, and say it's been stolen."

Think, Diane. Think. "Why shoot me? I've never been anything but nice to you."

"You were useful to do things for Mom when she was alive, but now that she's gone, there's no reason to leave you around. This evening your body will be discovered. After I've gotten over my grief at losing my mother and sister within the same month, I'll get all the estate. If my husband loses his job over his troubles ... well, I'll just have to divorce him and start over. Maybe in a tropical setting."

"Do you think you can just shoot me and get away with it?"

"Oh, I'll take some stuff to make it look like you walked in on a robber. Don't worry—although you'll be dead, so it won't matter."

"Will you take Bruce?"

"Oh, who cares? Let him go back to the pound. He's not important to me."

Diane knew she couldn't keep her sister talking forever. It occurred to her that this was the quandary that she'd written about. Now, as then, she didn't see a way out. But this was real. Meanwhile, Patricia's index finger was on the trigger, and she saw it grow white with tension. "Any final words?"

Diane dropped to her knees. "Please don't shoot. We can work this out."

Her sister's laugh had no mirth in it. "There's nothing to work out."

"Then let me at least say a final prayer."

Patricia hesitated, then nodded. "Make it fast."

Diane bowed her head, ostensibly to pray but in actuality to be certain of her position on the runner that was in her front hall. *If this doesn't work, at least I won't know it.* In one motion, she pulled the rug toward her, while rolling to her left to avoid the shot that she knew was coming. She tensed for the gunshot. but it never came. Patricia's head hit the corner of the entryway table as she went down, and she lay still, the revolver no longer in her hand.

Diane retrieved the revolver from where it lay. She made certain that her sister was out but still breathing, then pulled out her phone. She called 911, keeping a vigil on Patricia as she did. When her call was answered, she said, in a voice that was surprisingly calm, "Please send the police to my residence. An ambulance, too. My sister just tried to murder me." She gave the details, and hung on with the dispatcher, listening for the sirens to approach.

As she waited for the police response, Diane realized that not only did she have the ending to her medical mystery, but she had the outline almost complete in her head. Of course, no one would believe it. Then again, didn't they say that truth is stranger than fiction?

...

Joe sat at his desk, finishing some chart notes, his mind on automatic pilot. It had only been a month since Mrs. Macklin had died. Shortly after her death, Diane had found out that Wilma was responsible for it. Two weeks after she'd been charged with that murder, the elder sister, Patricia, was arrested for trying to shoot Diane, in order to get all of Ina Macklin's estate.

He'd offered commiseration for his fiancé, but had (wisely, he thought) not pushed her about moving forward. Let her get past all this before discussing future plans, no matter how anxious he was to get on with it. But a couple of weeks had passed since the episode with Patricia. It was time for Joe to approach Diane again.

"May I come in?"

Joe looked up and saw Diane standing in the open doorway of his office. "Of course. I was just thinking about you."

"No wonder my ears were burning," she said, as she closed the door and held out her arms for a hug. "Or maybe they weren't, since you weren't talking about me—just thinking."

The hug was accompanied by a kiss which seemed to last forever.

"Anyway, I'm glad to see you," said Joe when he finally came up for air. "How did work go today? This is the first day you've been back in the ER since Patricia held that gun on you."

"It went fine. I thought it would be good to get back to work, sort of get my mind off all the rest of the family stuff." she said.

"Sit down."

She took one of the two client chairs opposite his desk, and he took the other.

"So, what's on your mind?" he asked.

"You'll recall that, when we discussed moving ahead, I said that I was waiting for the other shoe to drop?"

"Yes."

"Well, it's dropped," she said. "My sister almost killed me, and I suppose that meets the definition of the other shoe. There may be more—something different, something we don't foresee—but I don't think we need to stand around and wait any longer. I think it's time for us to move ahead with our lives. Our life together."

Joe smiled—really smiled—for the first time in weeks. "I'm ready. Does this mean that we're 'going steady,' or whatever the kids call it?"

"I don't know what they call it. So far as I'm concerned, we've packed about half a year's worth of getting to know each other in the past few weeks. Now I'm ready to move on to whatever comes next."

He took her hand, but just then, there was a knock at his door.

"Yes?" he said.

It was his nurse. "Doctor Adams, we're about to check out and go home. Anything you need before we go?"

"You go ahead. Diane's with me." He looked over at her and smiled. "There's nothing we can't handle together. Nothing at all."

Books by Richard L. Mabry, MD

Novels of Medical Suspense
Code Blue
Medical Error
Diagnosis Death
Lethal Remedy
Stress Test
Heart Failure
Critical Condition
Fatal Trauma
Miracle Drug
Medical Judgment
Cardiac Event
Guarded Prognosis
Critical Decision
Novellas
Rx Murder
Silent Night, Deadly Night
Doctor's Dilemma
Surgeon's Choice
Emergency Case
Bitter Pill
Medical Mystery
Non-Fiction
The Tender Scar: Life After the Death of A Spouse

Enjoy this preview of Richard Mabry's next novel, **More than a Game**

PROLOGUE

"Mr. Merrick, have you made up your mind whether you want to play children's games, or be a physician and make something of your life?"

The stress of the moment drove the words of Ben's carefully prepared answer from his head. He froze, silent and immobile as a mongoose in front of a cobra.

Ferdinand C. Duncan, MD, FACS, Dean of the Southwestern Medical School, leaned back in his chair, clasped his hands over his vested and ample belly, and looked at Ben over the tops of his half-spectacles. His expression was composed and serious, a perfect poker face.

"Well, Mr. Merrick?" The question hung in the air.

"Sir, my days of trying to play professional baseball are over. I didn't have the talent to play, even at the minor league level, and now I'm ready to move on."

"So, you're sure you want to be a physician?" He emphasized the 'sure' just as if it had been in italics.

Ben realized the ball was in his court. "Yes, sir. I'm absolutely certain that I've been called to the practice of medicine."

The dean removed his glasses and gestured with them to emphasize his next point. "Young man, medicine is indeed a calling, and a high calling at that. However, I trust that you aren't basing your decision to enter medicine on what you've characterized as a calling."

Ben could have kicked himself. Sure, he'd felt a kind of calling to medicine—admittedly, maybe one that was made more real by his failure to make it as a pro baseball player. But right now, he didn't want to be thought of as some kind of religious nut by the man who held the key to his getting into this prestigious medical school.

He certainly didn't think of himself as highly religious. True, he was a Christian. At least he'd said all the right words and done the right things at the time. He'd always tried to be honest and fair in his dealings. But he wasn't sure there was time for religion in the science-driven world of his medical studies, and he tried to shy away from it as much as possible.

He'd heard no disembodied voice saying, "Ben, become a surgeon." It was more a matter of what his father expected of him. His father had always wanted him to become a surgeon, and he had almost hit the ceiling when Ben told him he wanted to accept the contract to play baseball.

Ben tried to redeem the moment. "Sir," he replied to the dean, "this is a decision that I've made after a great deal of careful thought. I haven't necessarily experienced any sort of divine call, but I do believe that we are given the ability to reason and make intelligent decisions. I've done just that, and medicine is where I belong."

"But—"

"I admit that I took a different path by signing that baseball contract after just a year of college, but after it became apparent that my path lay in another direction, I've buckled down to finish my pre-med studies. and you'll agree that I've done well."

The Dean just nodded. That's when Ben decided to unload the second barrel of his shotgun approach. "My father is a physician, a surgeon. I know the work that goes into practicing medicine, and I'm prepared to put forth that effort, given the chance."

The faintest trace of a smile flitted across the Dean's stone face. "Ah, yes. You're Robert Merrick's boy. Robert was one of our finest students. Everyone here remembers him. At least we know you come from good stock."

Ben flinched at this but managed a small smile of his own. "Thank you, sir."

Like Saint Peter turning to a new chapter in his record book, Dean Duncan closed the folder in front of him and opened the next one. Without looking up, he said, "You should hear from us within a few weeks. Please send in the next applicant."

1

Two out, top of the ninth, tying run on third base, winning run at second.

Ben Merrick pounded his glove. He balanced his weight on the balls of his feet, ready to move in any direction.

He risked a glance to check the position of the sun. Here in center field at Yankee Stadium, that deadly orange globe was a treacherous adversary for home team and visitors alike, able at any moment to turn a routine fly ball into a triple.

Before he could refocus his attention, he heard the unmistakable crack of bat meeting ball. The flurry of motion by the players on the field barely registered in his peripheral vision. He strained his sun-blinded eyes for a glimpse of the white sphere arcing into the afternoon sky. At last, he saw it off to his right, falling earthward at an alarming rate. He sprinted flat out toward it, then dived with glove outstretched, and while in midair he heard the crowd chanting his name.

"Ben, Ben, Ben..."

"Ben, Ben. Hey, fellow. Are you ready for me to pre-op the next patient?"

Dr. Ben Merrick gave a quick shake of his head and found that his Yankee pinstripes had been transformed into a gray-green scrub suit. Instead of standing in the hallowed confines of Yankee Stadium, he was surrounded by the sea-green tile that covered the walls in Operating Room Number Four of Dallas' Memorial Hospital.

Ben glanced toward the head of the table where the anesthesiologist, Dr. Rick Hinshaw, sat. "Sorry. Just thinking about something else for a moment. I guess my coffee level's a quart low. Yeah, go ahead and pre-op the next one."

Ben felt a brief wave of embarrassment for his momentary lapse into what surgeons sometimes called a "sterile trance." This quickly passed, as he realized that for many aspects of the surgery he performed, his hands could move on automatic pilot, going on with the actions learned through so many repetitions while his mind was a million miles away. Well, 1500 miles away, if his estimate of the distance involved was correct.

Anyway, it's only suturing the skin incision. And sewing up the skin's sort of like driving through Kansas. Boring, monotonous, and you can do it without thinking.

Rachel Burnett, the circulating nurse for today's cases, interrupted Ben's thoughts with a gentle, "Excuse me, Dr. Merrick."

Ben glanced up at her. "Yes?"

"Doctor," she continued, "when you're between cases, you have two messages. Please call Dr. Gates, and Nell at your office. Neither call is urgent."

Ben nodded to indicate he'd heard, then turned his attention back to this last stage of the surgery. He used a long straight needle trailing thin green suture material to bring the skin edges together with neat stitches. There was a rhythm to the work, perfected by many repetitions. Grasp the skin with fine-toothed forceps, place the stitch, bring the skin edges together just so, tie the knot, wait for the assistant to cut the suture, repeat the process.

Between stitches, Ben stole peeks at Rachel as she bustled about the operating room, doing all the things that were necessary to wind up this operation and prepare for the hernia repair scheduled to follow. If she was aware that she'd attracted his attention, she showed no sign of it.

Mark Newkirk, the surgical resident, clipped the trailing ends of the last stitch. "Nice job, Dr. Merrick."

Ben nodded to acknowledge the compliment. "Thanks for your help."

"Always happy to scrub with you. And this wasn't just a simple endoscopic procedure. It's nice to see one done this way for a change."

Ben stepped away from the table. "Mark, write the orders, I'll do the op note and talk to the family. Rachel, do you need anything else from me before I head for the recovery room?"

Rachel glanced up from her charting. "No sir. We're fine. I'll call you in the surgeon's lounge when we're ready for the next one."

It seemed a shame to Ben that the surgical cap and mask, together with a shapeless scrub dress, made Rachel's natural beauty almost impossible to discern. But he'd been fortunate enough to see her in street clothes, and his mind supplied the details. Coal-black hair, sparkling blue eyes, a full mouth, all combined to give her the face of a mischievous angel, while her figure turned the heads of most men and sparked just a bit of envy on the part of many women.

Three or four times, Ben had been on the verge of asking Rachel for a date. And each time, he'd chickened out. *I can tackle a bleeding ulcer. I can hit a ninety-mile an hour fastball. But I'm scared to death to ask that little slip of a girl for a date.*

Ben shook his head. He snapped off his gloves, tossed his mask into the trashcan, and grabbed the three by five card containing the patient's identifying data. His routine from this point onward usually followed a pattern. He would talk with the patient's family, going over the surgery and reminding them of the follow-up care needed. Then he'd go into the surgeon's lounge to dictate the operative note and return his phone calls. Finally, he'd allow himself five minutes to relax with a cup of coffee before starting the process all over again, this time with a hernia repair.

And tomorrow will be the same. And the day after that. And...

With an effort that was almost physical, Ben thrust the thoughts aside and focused on the task at hand. He'd need to make that phone call to the Chief of Staff after he'd finished talking with the patient's family. And he wasn't looking forward to that call. Oh, well.

He shrugged and pushed through the door into the waiting room.

2

"Dr. Merrick, returning Dr. Gates' call."

Ben wiggled around, trying to get comfortable. Not for the first time, he postulated that the chairs in the dictation cubicles were modeled after some medieval torture device. He figured they were designed to be as uncomfortable as possible, to get the surgeons out of the lounge as soon as their operative notes were dictated and their phone calls made.

"Ben. Thanks for getting back to me."

Ben gave up on any thought of comfort and levered himself out of the chair. He took advantage of the long phone cord and began to pace. *I think I know what's coming. Man, I'm sick of this.*

Ben tried to keep his tone civil. "Not much choice, was there, George? The Chief of Staff calls a junior surgeon. That call's going to get returned. And I'll bet I know what it's about."

"Easy, Ben, I'm on your side. I just wanted to let you know that the Executive Committee met last night. And your name came up ... again."

"And I can bet who brought it up. What was it this time?"

"The committee wondered if you didn't need a bit more supervision on your cases," Gates said.

"The committee, or Leonard Hall?" Ben asked, barely controlling his temper. "Was he still looking for revenge after I testified against him in that trial?"

"It doesn't matter who brought it up, or what his motivation was," Gates replied. "The motion didn't carry. I just wanted to warn you."

"Thanks . . . I guess."

Ben finally ended the conversation, but he continued in his mind. *Why am I in this profession, anyway? You sacrifice your personal life. You climb out of bed in the middle of the night to operate, knowing you'll probably never be paid. You work yourself sick, but no one is grateful, and every move you make is put under the microscope.*

He kicked the chair, only to discover that the result was painful for him, not for the chair. Ben sighed and tried to get his feelings under control while he dialed his next call. *No sense taking out my frustration on Nell.*

"Nell, it's me. What's up?"

"Far be it from me to interrupt your attempts to heal the sick and put some cash in your bank account, but I knew you'd want to know about this letter that just came in," she said.

Ben had reached an agreement with Nell that anything in the mail that appeared to be personal would be put on his desk unopened. That is, he had reached that agreement. Nell seemed to consider it non-binding, subject to constant reinterpretation, and (most of all) silly, since she already knew more about his personal affairs than anyone else, including his mother and father. She reminded him to make dinner reservations for his infrequent dates, to have his car washed, to pick up his cleaning. In general, she ran his life, and she did it so well that he had a hard time balking at what, by most other persons, might be considered intolerable interference.

"I know better than to say anything about your opening my personal mail. What's this one?"

"You got a letter from your friend, Mason Kirby. Wasn't he your roommate when you played minor league baseball?"

"That's right. I guess you do listen sometimes." Ben grinned. "I haven't thought about Mason for a good while. What did he say?"

"He'll be in town soon, probably staying several weeks, and he hoped you'd be able to get together."

Ben smiled at the thought of revisiting Mason. "Did he say more?"

"According to his letter, his law firm wants him to help defend your baseball hero, Buck Chandler."

The prospects of seeing Mason, maybe having a chance to see Buck again, gave a lift to Ben's sagging spirits. He didn't know what kind of jam Buck was in, but whatever it was, he knew that adding his contribution to Mason's defense, even if it was minimal, would offer relief from the funk he found himself in. "I'll call Mason when I get back in the office. Thanks, Nell."

"Dr. Merrick, we're ready for you in Room 4." Rachel's voice via the intercom brought Ben back to the present.

"On my way," he said to the disembodied voice. Then into the phone, he told Nell good-bye and hung up. Time to go back to work. But throughout the next case, one corner of his mind was turning over the question of why Mason was being sent from San Francisco to Dallas to assist in the defense of this case, and what he might contribute to that defense.

Made in the USA
Middletown, DE
16 July 2024

57404737R00064